# MY BOOK HOUSE
## *The Treasure Chest*

# The Treasure Chest

Here's a heigh and a ho! for the treasure chest,
    And a ho! for the pure, pure gold,
And a ho, heigh-ho! for the precious things,
    And the secret gems untold!

Here's a heigh and a ho! for the purpose strong,
    And the bold stout hearts that roam,
And sail the Seven Seas of Life,
    To bring such treasures home!

# The
# TREASURE CHEST
## of
## *MY* BOOKHOUSE

EDITED BY
*Olive Beaupré Miller*

PUBLISHERS
*The* BOOKHOUSE *for* CHILDREN
CHICAGO      TORONTO

———————————◆———————————

*Publishers of*

*My* BOOKHOUSE
*Six Volumes*

*My* TRAVELSHIP
*Three Volumes*

*My* BOOK *of* HISTORY
*Six Volumes*

———————————◆———————————

# THE TREASURE CHEST

## The Clocks of Rondaine*

### Frank R. Stockton

CENTURIES ago, there stood on the banks of a river a little town called Rondaine. The river was a long and winding stream which ran through different countries, and was sometimes narrow and swift, and sometimes broad and placid; sometimes hurrying through mountain passes, and again meandering quietly through fertile plains; in some places of a blue color and almost transparent, and in others of a dark and sombre hue; and so it changed until it threw itself into a warm, far-spreading sea.

But it was quite otherwise with the little town. As far back as anybody could remember, it had always been the same that it was at the time of our story; and the people who lived there could see no reason to suppose that it would ever be different from what it was then. It was a pleasant little town, its citizens were very happy; and why there should be any change in it, the most astute old man in all Rondaine could not have told you.

If Rondaine had been famed for anything at all, it would have been for the number of its clocks. It had many churches, some little ones in dark side streets, and some larger ones in wider avenues; and in the steeple of each of these churches there was a clock. There were town buildings, very old ones, which stood upon the great central square. Each of these had a tower, and in each tower was a clock. Then there were clocks at street corners, and two clocks in the market-place, and clocks over shop-doors, a clock at each end of the bridge, and several large clocks a little way out of town. Many of these clocks were fashioned in some quaint and curious way. In one of the largest a stone man came out and struck the hours with a stone hammer, while a stone woman struck the half hours with a stone broom; and in another an iron donkey kicked the hours on a bell behind him.

*From *Fanciful Tales;* copyright 1894, by Charles Scribner's Sons. By permission of the publishers.

It would be impossible to tell all the odd ways in which the clocks of Rondaine struck; but in one respect they were alike; they all did strike. The good people of the town would not have tolerated a clock which did not strike.

It was very interesting to lie awake in the night and hear the clocks of Rondaine strike. First would come a faint striking from one of the churches in the by-streets, a modest sound, as if the clock was not sure whether it was too early or not; then from another quarter would be heard a more confident clock striking the hour clearly and distinctly.

When they were quite ready, but not a moment before, the seven bells of the large church on the square would chime the hour; after which, at a respectful interval of time, the other church clocks of the town would strike. After the lapse of three or four minutes, the sound of all these bells seemed to wake up the stone man in the tower of the town building, and he struck the hour with his hammer. When this had been done, the other town-clocks felt at liberty to strike, and they did so. And when every sound had died away, so that he would be certain to be heard if there was any one awake to hear, it would be very likely that the iron donkey would kick out the hour on his bell. But there were times when he kicked before any of the clocks began to strike.

One by one the clocks on the street corners struck, the up-town ones first, and afterward those near the river. These were followed by the two clocks on the bridge, the one at the country end waiting until it was quite sure that the one at the town end had finished. Somewhat later would be heard the clock of Vougereau, an old country-house in the suburbs.

The very last clock to strike in Rondaine was one belonging to a little old lady with white hair, who lived in a little white house in one of the prettiest and cleanest streets in the town.

# THE TREASURE CHEST

Her clock was in a little white tower at the corner of her house, and was the only strictly private clock which was in the habit of making itself publicly heard. Long after every other clock had struck, and when there was every reason to believe that for some time nothing but half-hours would be heard in Rondaine, the old lady's clock would strike quickly and with a tone that said, "I know I am right, and I wish other people to know it."

In a small house which stood at a corner of two streets in the town there lived a young girl named Arla. For a year or more this young girl had been in the habit of waking up very early in the morning, sometimes long before daylight, and it had become a habit with her to lie and listen to the clocks. Her room was at the top of the house, and one of its windows opened to the west and another to the south, so that sounds entered from different quarters. Arla liked to leave these windows open so that the sounds of the clocks might come in.

Arla knew every clock by its tone, and she always made it a point to lie awake until she was positively sure that the last stroke of the clock at Vougereau had sounded; but it often happened that sleep overcame her before she heard the clock of the little old lady with white hair. It was so very long to wait for that!

It was not because she wanted to know the hour that Arla used to lie and listen to the clocks. She could tell this from her own little clock in her room. This little clock, which had been given to her when she was a small girl, not only struck the hours and half-hours and quarter-hours, but there was attached to it a very pretty contrivance which also told the time. On the front of the clock, just below the dial, was a sprig of a rosebush beautifully made of metal, and on this, just after the hour had sounded, there was a large green bud; at a quarter past the hour this bud opened a little, so that the red petals could be seen; fifteen minutes later it was a half-blown rose, and at a quarter of an hour more it was nearly full blown; just before the hour the rose opened to its fullest extent, and so remained until the clock had finished striking, when it immediately shut up into a great green bud. This clock was a great delight to Arla; for not only was it a very pleasant thing to watch the unfolding of the rose, but it was a continual satisfaction to her to think that her little clock always told her exactly what time it was, no matter what the other clocks of Rondaine might say.

Arla's father and mother were thrifty, industrious people, who were very fond of their daughter, and wished her to grow up a thoughtful, useful woman. In the very early morning, listening to the clocks of Rondaine or waiting for them, Arla did a great deal of thinking; and it so happened, on the morning of the day before Christmas, when the stars were bright and the air frosty, and every outside sound very clear and distinct, that Arla began to think of something which had never entered her mind before.

"How in the world," she said to herself, "do the people of Rondaine know when it is really Christmas? Christmas begins as soon as it is twelve o'clock on Christmas Eve; but as some of the people depend for the time upon one clock and some upon others, a great many of them cannot truly know when Christmas Day has really begun. Even some of the church clocks make people think that Christmas has come, when in reality it is yet the day before. And not one of them strikes at the right time. As for the iron donkey, I believe he kicks whenever he feels like it. And yet there are people who go by him! I know this, for they have told me so. But the little old lady with white hair is worse off than anybody else. Christmas must always come ever so long before she knows it."

With these thoughts on her mind, Arla could not go to sleep again. She heard all the clocks strike, and lay awake until her own little clock told her that she ought to get up. During this time she had made up her mind what she should do. There was yet one day before Christmas; and if the people of the town could be made to see in what a deplorable condition they were on account of the difference in their clocks, they might have time to set the matter right so that all the clocks should strike the correct hour, and everybody should know exactly when Christmas Day began. She was sure that the citizens had never given this matter proper thought; and it was quite natural that such should be the case, for it was not every one who was in the habit of lying awake in the very early morning; and in the daytime, with all the out-door noises, one could not hear all the clocks strike in Rondaine. Arla therefore thought that a great deal depended upon her, who knew exactly how this matter stood.

When she went down to breakfast she asked permission of her mother to take a day's holiday. As she was a good girl, and never neglected either her lessons or her tasks, her mother was quite willing to give her the day before Christmas in which she could do as she pleased.

The day was cool, but the sun shone brightly and the air was pleasant.  In the country around about Rondaine Christmas-time was not a very cold season.   Arla put on a warm cape and a pretty white hood, and started out gayly to attend to the business in hand.  Everybody in Rondaine knew her father and mother, and a great many of them knew her, so there was no reason why she should be afraid to go where she chose.  In one hand she carried a small covered basket in which she had placed her rose clock. The works of this little clock were regulated by a balance-wheel, like those of a watch, and therefore it could be carried about without stopping it.

The first place she visited was the church at which she and her parents always attended service. It was a small building in a little square at the bottom of a hill, and, to reach it, one had to go down a long flight of stone steps. When she entered the dimly lighted church, Arla soon saw the sacristan, a pleasant-faced little old man whom she knew very well.

"Good-morning, sir," said she. "Do you take care of the church clock?"

The sacristan was sweeping the stone pavements of the church, just inside the door. He stopped and leaned upon his broom. "Yes, my little friend," he said, "I take care of everything here except the souls of the people."

"Well, then," said Arla, "I think you ought to know that your clock is eleven minutes too fast. I came here to tell you that, so that you might change it, and make it strike properly."

The sacristan's eyes began to twinkle. He was a man of merry mood. "That is very good of you, little Arla; very good indeed. And, now that we are about it, isn't there something else you would like to change? What do you say to having these stone pillars put to one side, so that they may be out of the way of the people when they come in? Or those great beams in the roof—they might be turned over, and perhaps we might find that the upper side would look fresher than this lower part, which is somewhat time-stained, as you see? Or, for the matter of that, what do you say to having our clock-tower taken down and set out there in the square before the church door?

Then short-sighted people could see the time much better, don't you think?  Now tell me, shall we do all these things together, wise little friend?"

A tear or two came into Arla's eyes, but she made no answer.

"Good-morning, sir," she said, and went away.

"I suppose," she said to herself as she ran up the stone steps, "that he thought it would be too much trouble to climb to the top of the tower to set the clock right.  But that was no reason why he should make fun of me.  I don't like him as much as I used to."

The next church to which Arla went was a large one, and it was some time before she could find the sacristan.  At last she saw him in a side chapel at the upper end of the church, engaged in dusting some old books.  He was a large man, with a red face, and he turned around quickly, with a stern expression, as she entered.

"Please, sir," said Arla, "I came to tell you that your church clock is wrong.  It strikes from four to six minutes before it ought to.  It should be changed so that it will be sure to strike at the right time."

The face of the sacristan grew redder and twitched visibly at her remark.

"Do you know what I wish?" he almost shouted in reply.

"No, sir," answered Arla.

"I wish," he said, "that you were a boy, so that I might take you by the collar and soundly cuff your ears, for coming here to insult an officer of the church in the midst of his duties!  But, as you are a girl, I can only tell you to go away from here as rapidly and as quietly as you can, or I shall have to put you in the hands of the church authorities!"

# THE TREASURE CHEST

Arla was truly frightened, and although she did not run—for she knew that would not be proper in a church—she walked as fast as she could into the outer air.

"What a bad man," she then said to herself, "to be employed in a church! It surely is not known what sort of a person he is, or he would not be allowed to stay there a day!"

Arla thought she would not go to any more churches at present, for she did not know what sort of sacristans she might find in them.

"When the other clocks in the town all strike properly," she thought, "it is most likely they will see for themselves that their clocks are wrong, and they will have them changed."

She now made her way to the great square of the town, and entered the building at the top of which stood the stone man with his hammer. She found the doorkeeper in a little room by the side of the entrance. She knew where to go, for she had been there with her mother to ask permission to go up and see the stone man strike the hour with his hammer, and the stone woman strike the half-hour with her broom.

The doorkeeper was a grave, middle-aged man with spectacles; and, remembering what had just happened, Arla thought she would be careful how she spoke to him.

"If you please, sir," she said, with a curtsey, "I should like to say something to you. And I hope you will not be offended when I tell you that your clock is not quite right. Your stone man and your stone woman are both too slow; they sometimes strike as much as seven minutes after they ought to strike."

The man looked steadily at her through his spectacles.

"I thought," continued Arla, "that if this should be known to you, you would have the works of the stone man and the stone woman altered so that they might strike at the right time. They can be heard so far, you know, that it is very necessary they should not make mistakes."

"Child," said the man, with his spectacles still steadily fixed on her, "for one hundred and fifty-seven years the thunder and the lightning in time of storm have roared and flashed around that clock, and the sun in time of fair weather has shone upon it. In that century and a half and seven years men and women have lived and have died, and their children and their grandchildren and their great-grandchildren; kings and queens have passed, and one generation after another, many times. And yet, through all these years, that stone man and that stone woman have stood there, and in storm and in fair weather, by daylight or in the darkness of night, they have struck the hours and the half-hours. Of all things that one hundred and fifty-seven years ago were able to lift an arm to strike, they alone are left. And now you, a child of thirteen, or perhaps fourteen years, come to me and ask me to change that which has not been changed for a century and a half and seven years!"

Arla could answer nothing with those spectacles fixed upon her. They seemed to glare more and more as she looked at them. "Good-morning, sir," she said, dropping a curtsey as she moved backward toward the door. Reaching it, she turned and hurried into the street.

"If those stone people," she thought, "have not been altered in all these years, it is likely they would now be striking two or three hours out of the way! But I don't know. If they kept on going slow for more than a century they must have come around to the right hour sometimes. But they will have to strike ever and ever so much longer before they come around there again!"

Arla now walked on until she came to a street corner where a cobbler had a little shop. In the angle of the wall of the house, at the height of the second story, was a clock. This cobbler did not like the confined air and poor light of his shop, and whenever the weather allowed he always worked outside on the side-walk. To-day, although it was winter, the sun shone brightly on this side of the street, and he had put his bench outside, close to his door, and was sitting there, hard at work. When Arla stopped before him he looked up and said, cheerfully:

"Good-morning, Mistress Arla. Do you want them half-soled, or heeled, or a patch put on the toes?"

"My shoes do not need mending," said Arla. "I came to ask if you could tell me who has charge of the clock at this corner."

"I can easily do that," he said, "for I am the man. I am paid by the year, for winding it up and keeping it in order. The pay is not great; but if it were larger, more people might want it, and I might lose it; and if it were less how could I afford to do it at all? So I am satisfied."

"But you ought not to be entirely satisfied," said Arla, "for the clock does not keep good time. I know when it is striking, for it has a very jangling sound, and it is the most irregular clock in Rondaine. Sometimes it strikes as much as twenty-five minutes after the hour, and very often it does not strike at all."

The cobbler looked up at her with a smile. "I am sorry," he said, "that it has a jangling stroke, but the fashioning of clocks is not my trade, and I could not mend its sound with awl, hammer, or waxed-end. But it seems to me, my good maiden, that you never mended a pair of shoes."

"No, indeed!" said Arla; "I should do that even worse than you would make clocks."

"Never having mended shoes, then," said the cobbler, "you do not know what a grievous thing it is to have twelve o'clock, or six o'clock, or any other hour, in fact, come before you are ready for it. Now, I don't mind telling you, because I know you are too good to spoil the trade of a hard-working cobbler—and shoemaker too, whenever he gets the chance to be one—that when I have promised a customer that he shall have his shoes or his boots at a certain time of day, and that time is drawing near, and the end of the job is still somewhat distant, then do I skip up the stairway and set back the hands of the clock according to the work that has to be done. And when my customer comes I look up to the clock-face and I say to him, 'Glad to see you!' and then he will look up at the clock and will say, 'Yes, I am a little too soon;' and then, as likely as not, he will sit down on the door-step here by me and talk entertainingly; and it may happen that he will sit there without grumbling for many minutes after the clock has pointed out the hour at which the shoes were promised.

"Sometimes, when I have been much belated in beginning a job, I stop the clock altogether, for you can well see for yourself that it would not do to have it strike eleven when it is truly twelve. And so, if my man be willing to sit down, and our talk be very entertaining, the clock being above him where he cannot see it without stepping outward from the house, he may not notice that it is stopped. This once served me very well, for an old gentleman, over-testy and over-punctual, once came to me for his shoes, and looking up at the clock, which I had prepared for him, exclaimed, 'Bless me! I am much too early!' And he sat down by me for three-quarters of an hour, in which time I persuaded him that his shoes were far too much worn to be worth mending any more, and that he should have a new pair, which, afterward, I made."

"I do not believe it is right for you to do that," said Arla; "but even if you think so, there is no reason why your clock should go wrong at night, when so many people can hear it because of the stillness."

"Ah, no!" said the cobbler, "I do not object to the clock being as right as you please in the night; but when my day's work is done, I am in such a hurry to go home to my supper that I often forget to put the clock right, or to set it going if it is stopped.

# THE TREASURE CHEST

But so many things stop at night—such as the day itself—and so many things then go wrong such as the ways of evil-minded people —that I think you truly ought to pardon my poor clock."

"Then you will not consent," said Arla, "to make it go right?"

"I will do that with all cheerfulness," answered the cobbler, pulling out a pair of waxed-ends with a great jerk, "as soon as I can make myself go right. The most important thing should always be done first; and, surely, I am more important than a clock!" And he smiled with great good-humor.

Arla knew that it would be of no use to stand there any longer and talk with this cobbler. Turning to go, she said:

"When I bring you shoes to mend, you shall finish them by my clock, and not by yours."

"That will I, my good little Arla," said the cobbler, heartily. "They shall be finished by any clock in town, and five minutes before the hour, or no payment."

Arla now walked on until she came to the bridge over the river. It was a long, covered bridge, and by the entrance sat the bridgekeeper.

"Do you know, sir," said she, "that the clock at this end of your bridge does not keep the same time as the one at the other end? They are not so very different, but I have noticed this one is always done striking at least two minutes before the other begins."

The bridgekeeper looked at her with one eye, which was all he had.

"You are as wrong as anybody can be," said he. "I do not say anything about the striking, because my ears are not now good enough to hear the clock at the other end when I am near this one; but I know they both keep the same time. I have often looked at this clock and have then walked to the other end of the bridge, and have found that the clock there was exactly like it."

Arla looked at the poor old man, whose legs were warmly swaddled on account of rheumatism, and said:

"But it must take you a good while to walk to the other end of the bridge."

"Out upon you!" cried the bridgekeeper. "I am not so old as that yet! I can walk there in no time!"

Arla now crossed the bridge and went a short distance along a country road until she came to the great stone house known as Vougereau. This belonged to a rich family who seldom came there, and the place was in charge of an elderly man who was the brother of Arla's mother. When his niece was shown into a room on the ground floor, which served for his parlor and his office, he was very glad to see her; and while Arla was having something to eat and drink after her walk, the two had a pleasant chat.

"I came this time, Uncle Anton," she said, "not only to see you, but to tell you that the great clock in your tower does not keep good time."

Uncle Anton looked at her a little surprised.

"How do you know that, my dear?" he said.

Then Arla told him how she had lain awake in the early morning, and had heard the striking of the different clocks. "If you wish to make it right," said she, "I can give you the proper time, for I have brought my own little clock with me."

She was about to take her rose-clock out of her basket, when her uncle motioned to her not to do so.

"Let me tell you something," said he  "The altering of the

time of day, which you speak of so lightly, is a very serious matter, which should be considered with all gravity. If you set back a clock, even as little as ten minutes, you add that much to the time that has passed. The hour which has just gone by has been made seventy minutes long. Now, no human being has the right to add anything to the past, nor to make hours longer than they were originally made. And, on the other hand, if you set a clock forward even so little as ten minutes, you take away that much from the future, and you make the coming hour only fifty minutes long. Now, no human being has a right to take anything away from the future, or to make the hours shorter than they were intended to be. I desire, my dear niece, that you will earnestly think over what I have said, and I am sure that you will then see for yourself how unwise it would be to trifle with the length of the hours which make up our day. And now, Arla, let us talk of other things."

And so they talked of other things until Arla thought it was time to go. She saw there was something wrong in her uncle's reasoning, although she could not tell exactly what it was, and thinking about it, she slowly returned to the town. As she approached the house of the little old lady with white hair, she concluded to stop and speak to her about her clock. "She will surely be willing to alter that," said Arla, "for it is so very much out of the way."

The old lady knew who Arla was, and received her very kindly; but when she heard why the young girl had come to her, she flew into a passion.

"Never, since I was born," she said, "have I been spoken to like this! My great-grandfather lived in this house before me; that clock was good enough for him! My grandfather lived in this house before me; that clock was good enough for him! My father and mother lived in this home before me; that clock was good enough for them! I was born in this house, have always lived in it, and expect to die in it; that clock is good enough for me! And sooner than raise my hand against the clock of my ancestors, and the clock of my whole life, I would cut off that hand!"

Some tears came into Arla's eyes; she was a little frightened. "I hope you will pardon me, good madame," she said, "for, truly, I did not wish to offend you. Nor did I think that your clock is not a good one. I only meant that you should make it better; it is nearly an hour out of the way."

The sight of Arla's tears cooled the anger of the little old lady with white hair. "Child," she said, "you do not know what you are talking about, and I forgive you. But remember this: never ask persons as old as I am to alter the principles which have always made clear to them what they should do, or the clocks which have always told them when they should do it."

The poor girl now felt a good deal discouraged.

"The people don't seem to care whether their clocks are right or not," she said to herself, "and if they don't care, I am sure it is of no use for me to tell them about it. If even one clock could be made to go properly, it might help to make the people of Rondaine care to know exactly what time it is. Now, there is that iron donkey. If he would but kick at the right hour it would be an excellent thing, for he kicks so hard that he is heard all over the town."

Determined to make this one more effort, Arla walked quickly to the town-building, at the top of which was the clock with the iron donkey. This building was a sort of museum; it had a great many curious things in it, and it was in charge of a very ingenious man, who was learned and skilful in various ways.

# THE TREASURE CHEST

When Arla had informed the superintendent of the museum why she had come to him, he did not laugh at her nor did he get angry. He was accustomed to giving earnest consideration to matters of this sort, and he listened attentively to all that Arla had to say.

"You must know," he said, "that our iron donkey is a very complicated piece of mechanism. Not only must he kick out the hours, but five minutes before doing so he must turn his head around and look at the bell behind him; and then, when he has done kicking, he must put his head back into its former position. All this action requires a great many wheels and cogs and springs and levers, and these cannot be made to move with absolute regularity. When it is cold, some of the works contract; and when it is warm, they expand; and there are other reasons why he is very likely to lose or gain time. At noon, on every bright day, I set him right, being able to get the correct time from a sun-dial which stands in the court-yard. But his works—which I am sorry to say are not well made—are sure to get a great deal out of the way before I set him again."

"Then, if there are several cloudy or rainy days together, he goes very wrong indeed," said Arla.

"Yes, he truly does," replied the superintendent, "and I am sorry for it. But there is no way to help it except to make him all over again at my own expense, and that is something I cannot afford to do. The clock belongs to the town, and I am sure the citizens will not be willing to spend the money necessary for a new donkey-clock; for, so far as I know, every person but yourself is perfectly satisfied with this one."

"I suppose so," said Arla, with a sigh; "but it really is a great pity that every striking-clock in Rondaine should be wrong!"

"But how do you know they are all wrong?" asked the superintendent.

"Oh, that is easy enough," said Arla. "When I lie awake in the early morning, when all else is very still, I listen to their striking, and then I look at my own rose-clock to see what time it really is."

"Your rose-clock?" said the superintendent.

"This is it," said Arla, opening her basket and taking out her little clock.

The superintendent took it into his hands and looked at it attentively, both outside and inside. And then, still holding it, he stepped out into the court-yard. When in a few moments he returned, he said:

"I have compared your clock with my sun-dial, and find that it is ten minutes slow. I also see that, like the donkey, its works are not adjusted in such a way as to be unaffected by heat and cold."

"*My—clock—ten—minutes—slow!*" exclaimed Arla, with wide-open eyes.

"Yes," said the superintendent, "that is the case today, and on some days it is, probably, a great deal too fast. Such a clock as this—which is a very ingenious and beautiful one—ought frequently to be compared with a sun-dial or other correct time-keeper, and set to the proper hour. I see it requires a peculiar key with which to set it. Have you brought this with you?"

"No, sir," said Arla; "I did not suppose it would be needed."

"Well, then," said the superintendent, "you can set it forward ten minutes when you reach home; and if tomorrow morning you compare the other clocks with it, I think you will find that not all of them are wrong."

Arla sat quiet for a moment, and then she said: "I think I shall not care any more to compare the clocks of Rondaine with my little rose-clock. If the people are satisfied with their own clocks, whether they are fast or slow, and do not care to know exactly when Christmas Day begins, I can do nobody any good by listening to the different strikings and then looking at my own little clock, with a night-lamp by it."

"Especially," said the superintendent, with a smile, "when you are not sure that your rose-clock is right. But if you bring here your little clock and your key on any day when the sun is shining, I will set it to the time shadowed on the sun-dial, and show you how to do it yourself."

"Thank you very much," said Arla, and she took her leave.

As she walked home, she lifted the lid of her basket and looked at her little rose-clock. "To think of it!" she said. "That you should be sometimes too fast and sometimes too slow! And, worse than that, to think that some of the other clocks have been right and you have been wrong! But I do not feel like altering you today. If you go fast sometimes, and slow sometimes, you must be right sometimes, and one of these days, when I take you to be compared with the sun-dial, perhaps you will not have to be altered so much."

Arla went to bed that night quite tired with her long walks, and when she woke it was broad daylight. "I do not know," she said to herself, "exactly when Christmas began, but I am very sure that the happy day is here."

"Do you lie awake in the morning as much as you used to?" asked Arla's mother, a few weeks after the Christmas holidays.

"No, mother dear," said Arla; "I now sleep with one of my windows shut, and I am no longer awakened by that chilly feeling which used to come to me in the early morning, when I could draw the bed-covers close about me and think how wrong were the clocks of Rondaine."

And the little rose-clock never went to be compared with the sun-dial. "Perhaps you are right now," Arla would say to her clock each day when the sun shone, "and I will not take you until some time when I feel very sure that you are wrong."

## The Swineherd

HANS CHRISTIAN ANDERSEN

THERE was once a poor Prince; he had only quite a tiny kingdom, but it was big enough to allow him to marry, and he was bent upon marrying.

Now it certainly was rather bold of him to say to the Emperor's daughter, "Will you have me?" He did, however, venture to say so, for his name was known far and wide; and there were hundreds of Princesses who would have said "Yes," and "Thank you, kindly," but see if *she* would!

Just let us hear about it.

A rose tree grew on the grave of the Prince's father,—such a beautiful rose tree; it only bloomed every fifth year, and then only bore one blossom; but what a rose that was! By merely smelling it one forgot all one's cares and sorrows.

Then he had a nightingale which sang as if every lovely melody in the world dwelt in her little throat. This rose and this nightingale were to be given to the Princess, so they were put into great silver caskets and sent to her.

The Emperor had them carried before him into the great Hall where the Princess was playing at "visiting" with her ladies-in-waiting; they had nothing else to do. When she saw the caskets with the gifts she clapped her hands with delight.

"If only it were a little pussy cat!" said she,—but there was the lovely rose.

"Oh, how wonderfully it is made!" said all the ladies-in-waiting.

"It is more than beautiful," said the Emperor; "it is neat."

But the Princess touched it, and then she was ready to cry.

"Fie, papa!" she said; "it is not *made* at all, it is nothing but a *real* rose!"

"Fie," said all the ladies-in-waiting; "it is nothing but a *real* rose!"

# THE TREASURE CHEST

"Well, let us see what there is in the other casket, before we get angry," said the Emperor, and out came the nightingale. It sang so beautifully that at first no one could find anything to say against it.

"*Superbe! charmant!*" said the ladies-in-waiting, for they all chattered French, each one worse than the other.

"How that bird reminds me of our late Empress's musical box," said an old courtier. "Ah yes, they are the same tunes, and the same beautiful expression."

"So they are," said the Emperor, and he cried like a child.

"I should hardly think it could be a *real* bird," said the Princess.

"Yes, it is a real one," said those who had brought it.

"Then let it fly away," said the Princess, and she positively refused to see the Prince. But he was not to be discouraged; he stained his face brown and black, and, pulling his cap over his eyes, he knocked at the door.

"Good morning, Emperor," said he, "can I be taken into service in the palace?"

"Well, there are so many wishing to do that," said the Emperor, "but let me see!—yes, I need somebody to look after the pigs, for we have so many of them."

So the Prince was made imperial swineherd. A horrid little room was given him near the pig-sties, and here he had to live. The whole day long he sat busily at work, and by evening, he had made a beautiful little pot with bells all round it. When the pot boiled the bells rang out merrily and played the old tune:—

"*Alas, my darling Augustine!*
*All is lost, lost, lost!*"

But the most peculiar thing about it was, that by holding one's finger in the steam one could immediately smell what kind of meals were being cooked at every stove in the town. Now this was a very different matter from the rose.

The Princess came walking along with all her ladies-in-waiting, and when she heard the tune she stopped at once and looked greatly pleased for she, too, could play "Alas, my darling Augustine!" It was the only tune that she could play on the piano, and she played it with only one finger.

"Why, that is my tune," she said; "this must be a well educated swineherd. Listen, you must go in and ask him what the price of that instrument is."

So one of the ladies-in-waiting had to go in, but she put wooden shoes on first, so as not to soil her slippers.

"How much do you want for the pot?" she asked.

"I must have ten kisses from the Princess," said the swineherd.

"Mercy on us!" said the lady.

"I won't take less," said the swineherd.

"Well, what does he say?" asked the Princess.

"I really cannot tell you," said the lady-in-waiting, "it is too shocking."

"Then you must whisper it." And she whispered it.

"He is a wretch!" said the Princess, and went away at once. But she had only gone a little way when she heard the bells tinkling beautifully:

> "*Alas, my darling Augustine!*
> *All is lost, lost, lost!*"

"Go and ask him if he will take ten kisses from my ladies-in-waiting."

"No, thank you," said the swineherd; "ten kisses from the Princess, or I keep my pot."

"How tiresome it is," said the Princess. "Then you will have to stand round me, so that no one may see."

So the ladies-in-waiting stood round her and spread out their skirts while the swineherd took his ten kisses, and then the Princess got the pot.

# THE TREASURE CHEST

What a delight it was to them. The pot was kept on the boil day and night. They knew what was cooking on every stove in the town, from the chamberlain's to the shoemaker's. The ladies-in-waiting danced about and clapped their hands.

"We know who has sweet soup and pancakes for dinner, and who has cutlets; how amusing it is."

"Highly interesting," said the mistress of the robes.

"Yes, but you must keep the secret of how I got it, for I am the Emperor's daughter," said the Princess.

"Mercy on us! Quite so," they all answered.

The swineherd—that is to say, the Prince, only nobody knew that he was not a real swineherd—did not let the day pass in idleness, and he now constructed a rattle. When it was swung round it played all the waltzes, gallops and jig tunes which have ever been heard since the creation of the world.

"But this is *superbe!*" said the Princess, as she walked by. "I have never heard finer compositions. Go and ask him what the instrument costs, but let us have no more kissing."

"He wants a hundred kisses from the Princess!" said the lady-in-waiting.

"I think he is mad!" said the Princess, and she went away, but she had not gone far when she stopped.

"One must encourage art," she said; "I am the Emperor's daughter. Tell him he can have ten kisses, the same as yesterday, and he can take the others from the ladies-in-waiting."

"But we don't like that at all," said the ladies.

"Oh, nonsense! If I can kiss him you can do the same. Remember that I pay your wages as well as give you board and lodging." So the lady-in-waiting had to go to the swineherd again.

"A hundred kisses from the Princess," said he, "or let each keep his own."

"Stand in front of me then," said the Princess, and all the

ladies-in-waiting stood round, while the swineherd kissed her.

"Whatever is the meaning of that crowd round the pig-sties?" said the Emperor, who had stepped out on to the balcony. He rubbed his eyes and put on his spectacles. "Why it is the ladies-in-waiting! What game are they up to! I must go and see!" So he pulled up the heels of his slippers for they were shoes which he had trodden down.

Bless us, what a hurry he was in! When he got into the yard, he walked very softly and the ladies were so busy counting the kisses, so that there should be fair play, and neither too few nor too many kisses, that they never heard the Emperor. He stood on tiptoe.

"What is all this?" he said, when he saw that the swineherd and the Princess were kissing each other, and he thumped them on the head with his slipper just as the swineherd was taking the eighty-sixth kiss.

"Be off with you!" cried the Emperor, for he was furious, and on the spot he expelled both the Princess and the swineherd from his empire. There stood the Princess crying, and the rain poured down in torrents.

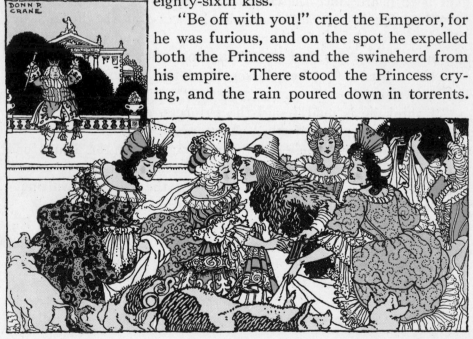

"Oh, miserable creature that I am!" cried the Princess, "if only I had accepted the handsome Prince who sent me the rose and the nightingale. Oh, how unhappy I am!"

But the swineherd went behind a tree, wiped the black and brown stain from his face, and threw away his ugly clothes. Then he came forward in princely attire, so handsome that the Princess could not help curtseying to him.

"Thou hast taught me to despise thee," he said. "Thou wouldst not have an honourable prince; thou couldst not value the *real* rose or the nightingale, but thou wouldst kiss a swineherd for the sake of a silly toy, a trumpery *made* musical box! As thou hast chosen, so must thou abide!"

Then he went back into his own little kingdom and shut and locked the door. So she had to stand outside and sing in earnest:

*"Alas, my darling Augustine!*
*All is lost, lost, lost!"*

### DEAR SENSIBILITY
Dear Sensibility, O la!
I heard a little lamb cry baa!
Says I, "So you have lost mama?"
      "Ah!"

The little lamb, as I said so,
Frisking about the field did go,
And frisking, trod upon my toe,
      "Oh!"
      —*Old Rhyme.*

## The Boy of Cadore*

### KATHERINE DUNLAP CATHER

THE boy's eyes were dark, and they gazed wistfully after the horseman who was dashing along the white highway.

"Think of it, Catarina!" he exclaimed. "He rides to the wonderful city."

Catarina looked at her brother as if she did not understand. There were many towns along the road that ribboned away to the south, each of which seemed large indeed to the mountain girl, yet she had never thought of them as wonderful.

"The wonderful city?" she repeated. "Where is that, Tiziano?"

"Why, don't you know?" he asked in surprise. "As if it could be other than Venice, the great city of St. Mark!"

But the name did not thrill black-eyed Catarina. Older than her brother, and far less of a dreamer, she had heard that dreadful things happened in the city, and that sometimes people went hungry there. In the mountains there was food enough and to spare, and though no one was rich and lived in a palace with tapestried walls and gorgeous furnishings, neither were there any very poor. So she shrugged her shoulders and replied: "Oh, Venice! I don't know why you call that wonderful. There are no mountains there, nor meadows where wild flowers grow. Are you tired of the Dolomites, Tiziano?"

"Ah, no!" came the earnest reply. "But the artists live in the city, and if I could go there, I might study with Bellini, and paint some of the things that are in my heart."

Catarina was just a practical village girl, who thought that if one had enough to eat and wear, he ought to be satisfied. So her voice was chiding and a bit impatient as she answered.

"You talk so much about painting, and seeing things no one else sees, that the villagers say unless you get over your dreaming

*From *Boyhood Stories of Famous Men*. Reprinted by the courteous permission of the publishers, The Century Company.

ways, you will grow up to be of no account. That is why Father thinks of apprenticing you to Luigi, the cobbler. For he can teach you his trade, which would be far better than always thinking about Venice. For, Tiziano, there are other things in the world beside painting."

Tiziano shook his head, but did not reply. Nothing else mattered half so much to him, and many a night, when the rest of the family were sleeping, he lay in his bed wondering how he could persuade his father to let him go away to study. It was well known that he spent many hours drawing on boards, stones, and anything he could find, and that the village priest, the good padrone, had praised his work. But little was thought of that. Other youths of Cadore had sketched as well and amounted to nothing. So why should he be sent to the city just because he could copy a mountain or a bit of woodland? For he could not make them understand that color was what seemed to burn in his soul, because that he could not express with charcoal.

A whistle came from down the road, and Catarina saw her brother Francesco beckoning them to hurry.

"They must be ready to begin weaving the garlands!" she exclaimed.

So they broke into a run toward the village inn.

It was the glowing, fragrant June time of the Italian highlands, when the hillsides and meadows of the fertile Dolomite valleys were masses of many colored bloom, and next day the Festival of Flowers was to take place. They had spent the afternoon blossom hunting, and now, when sunset was crimsoning the peaks, were homeward bound with their spoils, to aid in preparing for the revelry.

In a few minutes, they joined the other young people at the inn, and began making garlands, and planning games and frolics as they worked. Pieve di Cadore was very far from the world in those days of little travel, and when the time of a festival was at hand, the villagers were as light-hearted as the gay Venetians at carnival time. Songs and merry jests went round.

"Have you heard that Salvator, the miller's son, is going to Venice to study the art of carving?" asked a girl whose tongue kept pace with her hands. "Since his father has become rich, he has given up the idea of having him follow his own trade, and thinks it more elegant to become a sculptor."

Sebastiano, whose uncle was a lawyer's clerk in Bergamo, and who knew more of city ways than the other village youths, remarked: "I didn't know he had the love of carving. It takes something beside a rich father to make an artist."

The talkative girl tossed her head.

"That may be!" she retorted. "But no money, no masters, and without them, pray, how can one do anything?"

"So I tell Tiziano when he talks about going to the city to study painting," Catarina broke in. "Father is not rich, and it would be better for him to think of learning cobbling with Luigi."

Peals of laughter followed the announcement, and some one called out, "Tiziano! Why, he hasn't had even a drawing-master. He builds the tower of his castle before the foundation."

Tiziano's face turned red. He had no teacher, it was true. But he believed he could prove he was worth one if given a chance.

"Oh, if I only had some paints!" he thought. "Maybe they would stop calling me a dreamer, for I am sure I could make a picture, and then perhaps I could go."

But pigments were rare and costly, and though his father was a well-to-do mountaineer, he had no gold to waste in buying colors for a lad who had never been taught to use them.

The next morning, the boy noticed stains on the stone walk made by flowers crushed there the day before. They were bright and fresh as if painted, and it put an idea into his head. He did not speak of it, however, although it was on his mind so much

that, when the gaily decked villagers danced on the green, he did not see them, but, as soon as a chance came, he crept from the revelers and went out into the meadows.

Catarina saw him go, and wondered what took him from the merriment. Her curiosity was greater than her desire for fun, so she followed, and overtook him just as he reached a hillside aglow with blossoms.

"What are you doing, Tiziano?" she called.

The boy looked up as if doubtful whether to tell or not. But he knew his sister loved him even though she did criticize his dreaming, and that she would keep his secret.

"I am going to paint a picture," he answered.

For a minute she stood and stared. Then, thinking he was teasing, she retorted: "Of course you are, without any paints!"

But his earnest face told he was not joking.

"I shall use blossoms," he continued, with a wonderful light in his eyes. "See, all the colors are here, and I have found that they will stain. I saw where they did it on the stone walk."

Catarina was not a dreamer like her brother, and never saw pictures where others found only a bit of color, but she believed that what he proposed to do was not impossible, for she too had noticed the stains on the stone. And she began to think that he must be a very bright lad, for no ordinary one would have thought of it, and that perhaps his wanting to go to Venice was not a wild idea after all. She had heard the padrone say that no undertaking that fills the heart is impossible to one who has patience and courage and persistence, and that help always comes to those who try to help themselves. So she decided to help Tiziano, even though it was only in the keeping of his secret and the gathering of materials for the work.

So into the fragrant patches they went and began collecting blossoms of every hue—reds, pinks, blues, and purples such as sunset painted on the mountains, and warm yellows and lavenders that the boy saw in the pictures of his fancy. Then they hurried to an old stone house that stood on land owned by their father. It was a vacant house, seldom visited by the family, and never by the villagers, and there, where he would be safe from molestation, he was to paint the picture that they hoped would be the means of taking him to Venice. Catarina wanted to stay and watch the work, but Tiziano objected.

"I don't want even you to see it until it is finished, because at first it will not seem like a picture."

So she went away and left him outlining with a bit of charcoal on the wall.

For many days afterward, whenever he could steal away without being noticed, he worked with his flower paints. Catarina went over the meadows on feet that seemed to be winged, always watching that none of the villagers saw her put the blossoms in at the window near which her brother worked. So, while each petal made only a tiny stain, and the boy painted with the rapidity of one inspired, he not once needed to stop for materials.

Little by little the picture grew beneath the magic of his touch, and he and Catarina kept the secret well. Only the flocks pasturing on the fragrant uplands went near the deserted house, so no one knew that a boy was at work there who was destined to win glory for Italy. Little did the villagers dream, as Catarina skipped over the meadows, that the blossoms she gathered were being put to an immortal use.

One evening, when the sun was dipping behind the peaks and the merry voices of shepherds homeward bound with their flocks sounded down from the heights, Tiziano stepped to the door of the house and called to his sister outside:

"It is finished, Catarina, and is the very best that I can do!"

She went dancing in, filled with joy that the task was done, but when she stood in front of the picture, the merriment went out of her face, and she spoke in tones of reverence:

"Oh, Tiziano, a madonna!"

"Yes," he agreed. "A madonna and child, with a boy like me offering a gift. It is what was in my heart, Catarina."

For some minutes she stood there forgetting everything else in the beauty of the fresco. Then, thinking of what it would mean to her brother when the villagers knew he had done such a wonderful thing, she started out to spread the news.

"Come and see!" she called to Luigi, the cobbler, as she hurried past the door where he was sorting his leather. "Tiziano has painted a madonna on the walls of the old stone house."

Word travels fast when it goes by the tongues of villagers, and soon a group of folk moved toward the building where the lad waited. His father, coming down from a day's hunting in the mountains, saw them go, and followed, wondering what was the matter. But by the time he reached the place, such a crowd had gathered that he could not see the fresco.

Murmurs of "How did he do it?" "Where did he get his paints?" rose on all sides, and every one was so excited that the father could not find out why they were there. Then he heard Tiziano's voice: "I did it with flowers from the hillsides. Catarina gathered them while I worked."

Exclamations of amazement followed, and the good padrone

spoke reverently: "With the juices of flowers! Il divino Tiziano!"

Antonio Vecelli looked about him as if dazed, for he could not believe what he heard.

"Am I mad," he asked a villager who was standing close by, "or did the padrone call my Tiziano 'the divine'?"

"No," came the answer. "You are not mad."

And when they told him the story, and the crowd stepped back that he might see, he, too, thought it a wonderful thing.

Whether or not Salvator, the miller's son, went to the city to study sculpture, no one knows. But Tiziano did go, and the boy of Cadore became the marvel of Venice. There, guided by the master hand of Bellini, he began plying the brushes that were busy for almost eighty years, painting pictures whose glorious coloring has never been equaled, and proving to the mountain folk that it isn't bad, after all, to be a dreamer, for dreams combined with work do marvelous things. And if the father who thought he had gone mad when the village priest spoke his boy's name as reverently as he would a saint's, could come again to-day to the valley of flowers in the Italian highlands, he would hear the selfsame words that were used that twilight time in speaking of his lad.

"Ecco!" the villagers say, as they point to a noble statue that looks out toward the meadows in which Catarina gathered blossoms, "Il divino Tiziano.—See, the divine Titian!"

And by that name the world knows him to this very day.

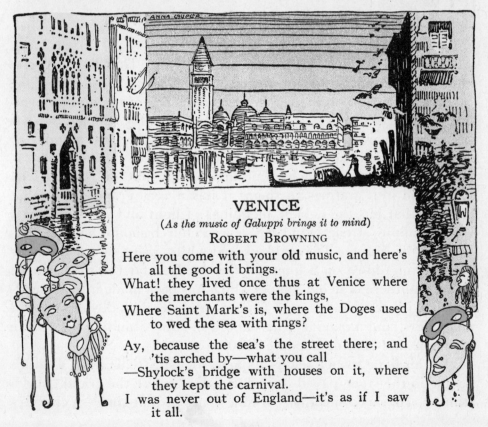

## VENICE

*(As the music of Galuppi brings it to mind)*

ROBERT BROWNING

Here you come with your old music, and here's
   all the good it brings.
What! they lived once thus at Venice where
   the merchants were the kings,
Where Saint Mark's is, where the Doges used
   to wed the sea with rings?

Ay, because the sea's the street there; and
   'tis arched by—what you call
—Shylock's bridge with houses on it, where
   they kept the carnival.
I was never out of England—it's as if I saw
   it all.

## The Nuremberg Stove
### LOUISE DE LA RAMEE

August lived in a little town called Hall.  Hall is a favorite name for several towns in Austria and Germany; but this one especial little Hall, in the Upper Innthal, is one of the most charming Old-World places that I know, and August for his part did not know any other.  It has the green meadows and the great mountains all about it, and the gray-green glacier-fed water rushes by it.  It has paved streets and enchanting little shops that have all latticed panes and iron gratings to them; it has a very grand old Gothic church, that has the noblest blendings of light and shadow, and a look of infinite strength and repose as a church should have.  Then there is the Muntze Tower, black and white, rising out of greenery and looking down on a long wooden bridge and the broad rapid river; and there is an old schloss which has been made into a guard-house, with battlements and frescoes and heraldic devices in gold and colors, and a man-at-arms carved in stone standing life-size in his niche and bearing his date 1530.

In this little town a few years ago August Strehla lived with his people in the stone-paved irregular square where the grand church stands.  He was a small boy of nine years at that time—a chubby-

# THE TREASURE CHEST

faced little man with rosy cheeks, big hazel eyes, and clusters of curls the brown of ripe nuts. His mother was dead, his father was poor, and there were many mouths at home to feed.

In this country the winters are long and very cold, and this night was terribly cold and dreary. The good burghers of Hall had shut their double shutters, and the few lamps there were, flickered dully behind their quaint, old-fashioned iron casings. The mountains indeed were beautiful, all snow-white under the stars. Hardly any one was astir; a few good souls wending home from vespers, a tired post-boy who blew a shrill blast from his tasselled horn as he pulled up his sledge before a hostelry, and little August, were all who were abroad, for the snow fell heavily and the good folks of Hall go early to their beds. He was half frozen and a little frightened, but he kept up his courage by saying over and over again to himself, "I shall soon be at home with dear Hirschvogel."

He went on through the streets into the place where the great church was, and where near it stood his father's house with the Pilgrimage of the Three Kings painted on its wall.

The snow outlined with white every gable and cornice of the beautiful old wooden houses; the moonlight shone on the gilded signs, the lambs, the grapes, the eagles, and all the quaint devices that hung before the doors. Here and there, where a shutter had not been closed, a ruddy fire-light lit up a homely interior, with the noisy band of children clustering round the house-mother and a big brown loaf, while the oilwicks glimmered, and the hearth-logs blazed, and the chestnuts sputtered in their iron roasting-pot. At August's knock the solid oak door of his father's home, four centuries old if one, flew open, and the boy darted in.

It was a large barren room into which he rushed with so much pleasure, and the bricks were bare and uneven. It had a walnut-wood press, handsome and very old, a broad deal table, and several wooden stools for all its furniture; but at the top of the chamber,

sending out warmth and color together as the lamp shed its rays upon it, was a tower of porcelain, burnished with all the hues of a king's peacock and a queen's jewels, and surmounted with armed figures, and shields, and flowers of heraldry, and a great golden crown upon the highest summit of all.

It was a stove of 1532, and on it were the letters H. R. H., for it was the handwork of the great potter of Nuremberg, Augustin Hirschvogel, who put his mark thus, as all the world knows.

The stove no doubt had stood in palaces and been made for princes, had warmed the crimson stockings of cardinals and the gold-broidered shoes of archduchesses; no one knew what it had seen or done or been fashioned for; but it was a right royal thing. Yet perhaps it had never been more useful than it was now in this poor desolate room, sending down heat and comfort into the troop of children tumbled together on a wolf-skin at its feet.

286

# THE TREASURE CHEST

"Oh, dear Hirschvogel, I am so cold, so cold!" said August, kissing its gilded lion's claws. "Is father not in, Dorothea?"

"No, dear. He is late."

Dorothea was a girl of seventeen, dark-haired and serious. She was the eldest of the Strehla family; and there were ten of them in all. Next to her there came Jan and Karl and Otho, big lads, gaining a little for their own living; and then came August, who went up in the summer to the high Alps with the farmers' cattle, but in winter could do nothing; and then all the little ones, who could only open their mouths to be fed like young birds—Albrecht and Hilda, and Waldo and Christof, and last of all little three-year-old Ermengilda, with eyes like forget-me-nots.

They were of that mixed race, half Austrian, half Italian, so common in the Tyrol; some of the children were white and golden as lilies, others were brown and brilliant as fresh-fallen chestnuts. The father was a good man, but weak and weary with so many to find food for and so little to do it with. He worked at the salt-furnaces, and by that gained a few florins. Dorothea was one of those maidens who almost work miracles, so far can their industry and care and intelligence make a home sweet and wholesome. Still, very poor they were, and Dorothea's heart ached with shame, for she knew that their father's debts were many for flour and meat and clothing. Of fuel to feed the big stove they had always enough without cost, for their mother's father was alive, and sold wood and fir cones and coke, and never grudged them to his grandchildren.

"Father says we are never to wait for him; we will have supper, now you have come home, dear," said Dorothea.

Supper was a huge bowl of soup, with big slices of brown bread swimming in it and some onions bobbing up and down; the bowl was soon emptied by ten wooden spoons, and then the three eldest boys slipped off to bed, being tired with their rough bodily labor in the snow all day. Dorothea drew her spinning-wheel by the stove and set it whirring, and the little ones got August down upon the old worn wolf-skin and clamored to him for a picture or a story.  For August was the artist of the family.

He had a piece of planed deal that his father had given him, and some sticks of charcoal, and he would draw a hundred things he had seen in the day—faces and dogs' heads, and men in sledges, and old women in their furs, and pine-trees, and cocks and hens, and all sorts of animals, and now and then—very reverently—a Madonna and Child. It was all very rough, for there was no one to teach him anything.  But it was all life-like, and kept the whole troop of children shrieking with laughter, or watching breathless, with wide open, wondering eyes.

They were all so happy; what did they care for the snow outside?  Their little bodies were warm, and their hearts merry; even Dorothea, troubled about the bread for the morrow, laughed as she spun; and August, with all his soul in his work, cried, as he looked at the stove that was shedding its heat on them all:

"Oh, dear Hirschvogel! you are almost as great and good as the sun! No; you are greater and better, I think, because he goes away nobody knows where all these long, dark, cold hours; but you— you are always ready; just a little bit of wood to feed you, and you will make a summer for us all the winter through!"

The grand old stove seemed to smile through all its iridescent surface at the praises of the child.  No doubt, though it had known three centuries and more, it had known but very little gratitude.

It was one of those magnificent stoves in enamel, of great height and breadth, with all the majolica lustre which Hirschvogel learned to give to his enamels.  There was the statue of a king at each corner.  The body of the stove itself was divided into panels, which had the Ages of Man painted on them; the borders of the panels had roses and holly and laurel and other foliage, and German mottoes in black letters.  The whole was burnished with gilding in many

parts, and was radiant everywhere with that brilliant coloring of which the Hirschvogel family were all masters.

Nothing was known of the stove at this latter day in Hall. The grandfather Strehla, who had been a master-mason, had dug it up out of some ruins where he was building, and, finding it without a flaw, had taken it home, and only thought it worth finding because it was such a good one to burn. That was now sixty years past, and ever since then the stove had stood in the big, desolate, empty room, warming three generations of the Strehla family, and having seen nothing prettier perhaps in all its many years than the children tumbled now in a cluster, like gathered flowers, at its feet.

To the children the stove was a household god. In summer they laid a mat of fresh moss all round it, and dressed it up with green boughs and the numberless beautiful wild flowers of the Tyrol country. In winter all their joys centered in it, and scampering home from school over the ice and snow, they were happy, knowing that they would soon be cracking nuts or roasting chestnuts in the broad ardent glow of its noble tower, which rose eight feet high above them with all its spires and pinnacles and crowns.

Once a traveling peddler had told them that the letters on it meant Augustin Hirschvogel, and that Hirschvogel had been a great German potter and painter, in the city of Nuremberg, and had made many such stoves that were all miracles of beauty, putting all his heart and soul into his labors, as the men of those earlier ages did, and thinking but little of gold or praise.

So the stove had got to be called Hirschvogel in the family, as if it were a living creature, and little August was very proud because he had been named after that famous old German who had had the genius to make so glorious a thing. All the children loved the stove, but with August the love of it was a passion; and in his secret heart he used to say to himself, "When I am a man, I will make just such things, and then I will set Hirschvogel in a beautiful house that I will build myself. That is what I will do."

For August, a salt-baker's son and a little cow-keeper when he was anything, was a dreamer of dreams, and when he was upon the high Alps with his cattle, with the stillness and the sky around him, was quite certain that he would live for greater things than driving the herds up when the spring-tide came among the blue sea of gentians, or toiling down in the town with wood and with timber as his father and grandfather did every day of their lives. He was a strong and healthy little fellow, as active as a squirrel and as playful as a hare. But he was always thinking, thinking, for all that.

August lay now in the warmth of the stove and told the children stories, his own little brown face growing red with excitement. That human being on the panels had always had the most intense interest for August, and he had made, not one history for him, but a thousand; he seldom told them the same tale twice.

# THE TREASURE CHEST

In the midst of their chatter and laughter a blast of frozen air and a spray of driven snow struck like ice through the room, and reached them even in the warmth of the old wolf-skins and the great stove. It was the door which had opened and let in the cold; it was their father who had come home. The younger children ran joyous to meet him, Dorothea pushed the one wooden arm-chair of the room to the stove, and August flew to set the jug of beer on a little round table, and fill a long clay pipe; for their father was good to them all, and they had been trained by the mother they had loved to dutifulness and obedience and a watchful affection.

Tonight Karl Strehla responded very wearily to the young ones' welcome, and came to the wooden chair with a tired step and sat down heavily, not noticing either pipe or beer. He was a fair, tall man, gray before his time, and bowed with labor.

"Take the children to bed," he said, suddenly, and Dorothea obeyed. August stayed behind, curled before the stove.

When Dorothea came down again, the cuckoo-clock in the corner struck eight; she looked to her father and the untouched pipe, then sat down to her spinning, saying nothing.

There was a long silence; the cuckoo called the quarter twice; August dropped asleep; Dorothea's wheel hummed like a cat.

Suddenly Karl Strehla struck his hand on the table, sending the pipe on the ground.

"I have sold Hirschvogel," he said; and his voice was husky and ashamed in his throat. The spinning-wheel stopped. August sprang erect out of his sleep.

"Sold Hirschvogel!"

"I have sold Hirschvogel!" said Karl Strehla, in the same husky, dogged voice. "I have sold it to a traveling trader for two hundred florins. What would you?—I owe double that. He saw it this morning when you were all out. He will pack it and take it to Munich tomorrow."

Dorothea gave a low shrill cry: "Oh, father!—the children—in mid-winter!" She turned white as the snow without.

August stood, half blind with sleep, staring with dazed eyes.

"It is not true?" he muttered. "You are jesting, father?"

Strehla broke into a dreary laugh.

"It is true. Would you like to know what is true too?—that the bread you eat, and the meat you put in this pot, and the roof you have over your heads, are none of them paid for. If it had not been for your grandfather, I should have been in prison all summer and autumn, and he is out of patience and will do no more now. Boy, you stare at me as if I were a mad dog! You have made a god of yon china thing. Well,—it goes: goes tomorrow!"

August stood like a creature paralyzed.

"It is not true!" he echoed, stupidly.

"You will find it true," said his father, doggedly, and angered because he was in his own soul bitterly ashamed to have bartered away the heirloom and treasure of his race and the comfort of his young children. "The dealer has paid me half the money tonight, and will pay me the other half tomorrow. The little black stove in the kitchen will warm you all just as well. Who would keep a gilded, painted thing in a poor house like this, when one can make two hundred florins by it? What is it, when all is said?—a bit of hardware much too grand-looking for such a room as this."

August gave a shriek, and threw himself at his father's feet.

"Oh, father!" he cried, his hands closing on Strehla's knees. "You cannot mean what you say? Send *it* away—our life, our sun, our joy, our comfort? You could not do such a thing. It is not a piece of hardware; it is a living thing, and it loves us though we are only poor little children, and we love it with all our hearts and souls! Oh, listen; I will go and try and get work tomorrow! I will ask them to let me cut ice or make the paths through the snow. And I will beg the people we owe money to to wait; they are all

# THE TREASURE CHEST

neighbors, they will be patient. But sell Hirschvogel!—oh, never! Give the florins back to the man. Oh, father, do hear me, for pity's sake!"

Strehla was moved by the boy's anguish. He loved his children, and their pain was pain to him. But stronger than emotion, was the anger that August roused in him; he hated and despised himself for the barter of the heirloom of his race, and every word of the child stung him with a stinging sense of shame.

And he spoke in his wrath rather than in his sorrow.

"You are a little fool," he said, harshly, as they had never heard him speak. "Get up and go to bed. There is no more to be said. Children like you have nothing to do with such matters. The stove is sold, and goes to Munich tomorrow. What is it to you? Be

thankful I can get bread for you.  Get on your legs, I say, and go to bed."

Then Strehla took the oil-lamp that stood at his elbow and stumbled off to his own chamber.

August laughed aloud; then all at once his laughter broke down into bitterest weeping.  He threw himself forward on the stove, covering it with kisses, and sobbing as though his heart would burst from his bosom.  What could he do?  Nothing, nothing, nothing!

"August, dear August," whispered Dorothea, piteously, and trembling all over,—for she was a very gentle girl, and fierce feeling terrified her,—"August, do not lie there.  Come to bed.  In the morning you will be calmer.  It is horrible indeed, but if it be father's will—"

"Let me alone," said August through his teeth, striving to still the storm of sobs that shook him from head to foot.  "Let me alone. In the morning!—how can you speak of the morning?"

"Come to bed, dear," sighed his sister.  "Oh, August, do not lie and look like that! you frighten me.  Do come to bed."

"I shall stay here."

"Here! all night!"

"They might take it in the night.  Besides, to leave it *now!*"

"But it is cold! the fire is out."

"It will never be warm any more, nor shall we."

All his childhood had gone out of him, all his gleeful, careless, sunny temper had gone with it; he spoke sullenly and wearily, choking down the great sobs in his chest.  To him it was as if the end of the world had come.

His sister lingered by him while striving to persuade him to go to his place in the little crowded bed chamber with Albrecht and Waldo and Christof.  But it was in vain.  "I shall stay here," was all he answered her.  And he stayed—all the night long.

The lamps went out; the rats came and ran across the floor;

as the hours crept on through midnight and past, the cold intensified and the air of the room grew like ice. August did not move; he lay with his face downward on the golden and rainbow-hued pedestal of the household treasure, which henceforth was to be cold for evermore, an exiled thing in a far off land.

Whilst yet it was dark his three elder brothers came down the stairs and let themselves out, each bearing his lantern and going to his work in stone-yard and timber-yard and at the saltworks. They did not notice him; they did not know what had happened.

A little later his sister came down with a light in her hand to make ready the house ere morning should break.

She stole up to him and laid her hand on his shoulder timidly.

"Dear August, you must be frozen. August, do look up! do speak! It is morning, only so dark!"

August shuddered all over. "The morning!" he echoed. He slowly rose up to his feet. "I will go to grandfather," he said, very low. "He is always good; perhaps he could save it."

Loud blows with the heavy iron knocker of the house-door drowned his words. A strange voice called aloud through the keyhole: "Let me in! Quick!—there is no time to lose! More snow like this, and the roads will all be blocked. Let me in! Do you hear? I am come to take the great stove."

August sprang erect, his fists doubled, his eyes blazing.

"You shall never touch it!" he screamed; "you shall never touch it!"

"Who shall prevent us?" laughed a big man, who was a Bavarian, amused at the fierce little figure fronting him.

"I!" said August. "You shall never have it!"

"Strehla," said the big man, as August's father entered the room, "you have got a little mad dog here; muzzle him."

One way and another they did muzzle him. He fought like a little demon, and hit out right and left. But he was soon mastered by four grown men, and his father flung him with no light hand out from the door of the back entrance, and the buyers of the stately and beautiful stove set to work to pack it heedfully and carry it away.

When Dorothea stole out to look for August, he was nowhere in sight. She went back to little 'Gilda, and sobbed, whilst the others stood looking on, dimly understanding that with Hirschvogel was going all the warmth of their bodies, all the light of their hearth. In another moment Hirschvogel was gone—gone forever and aye.

August had stood still for a time, leaning against the back wall of the house. The wall looked on a court where a well was. Into the court an old neighbor hobbled for water, and, seeing the boy, said: "Child, is it true your father is selling the big stove?"

August nodded his head, then burst into a passion of tears.

"Well, for sure he is a fool," said the neighbor. "Heaven forgive me for calling him so before his own child! but the stove was worth a mint of money. If sell it he must, he should have taken it to good Herr Steiner over at Spruz, who would have given him honest value. But if I were you I would do better than cry. I would go after it."

Then the old man hobbled away.

August remained leaning against the wall; his head was buzzing and his heart fluttered with the new idea which had presented itself to his mind. "Go after it," had said the old man. He thought, "Why not go with it?"

He was by this time in that state of exaltation in which the impossible looks quite natural and commonplace. He ran out of the court-yard, and across to the huge Gothic porch of the church. From there he could watch unseen his father's door.

Presently his heart gave a great leap, for he saw the straw-enwrapped stove brought out and laid with infinite care on the bullock dray. Two of the Bavarian men mounted beside it, and

# THE TREASURE CHEST

the sleigh-wagon slowly crept over the snow of the place. The noble old minster looked its grandest and most solemn, with its dark-gray stone and its vast archways, and its strange gargoyles and lamp-irons black against the snow; but for once August had no eyes for it: he only watched for his old friend. Then he, a little unnoticeable figure enough, like a score of other boys in Hall, crept, unseen by any of his brothers or sisters, out of the porch and followed in the wake of the dray.

Its course lay towards the station of the railway. August heard the Bavarians arguing a great deal, and learned that they meant to go too and wanted to go with the great stove itself. But this they could not do, for neither could the stove go by a passenger-train nor they themselves go in a goods-train. So at length they insured their precious burden for a large sum, and consented to send it by a luggage-train which was to pass through Hall in half an hour.

August heard, and a desperate resolve made itself up in his little mind. Where Hirschvogel went, would he go. He gave one terrible thought to Dorothea—poor, gentle Dorothea!—sitting in the cold at home, then set to work to execute his project. How he managed it he never knew very clearly himself, but certain it is that when the goods-train from the north moved out of Hall, August was hidden behind the stove in the great covered truck, and wedged, unseen and undreamt of by any human creature, amidst the cases of wood-carving, of clocks, of Vienna toys, of Turkish carpets, of Russian skins, which shared the same abode as did his swathed and bound Hirschvogel.

It was very dark in the closed truck, which had only a little window above the door. But August was not frightened; he was close to Hirschvogel, and presently he meant to be closer still; for he meant to do nothing less than get inside Hirschvogel itself. Being a shrewd little boy, and having had by great luck two silver groschen in his breeches-pocket, which he had earned the day before by chopping wood, he had bought some bread and sausage at the station of a woman there who knew him, and who thought he was going out to his uncle Joachim's chalet above Jenbach. This he ate in the darkness.

When he had eaten, he set to work like a little mouse to make a hole in the withes of straw and hay which enveloped the stove. He gnawed, and nibbled, and pulled, and pushed, making his hole where he guessed that the opening of the stove was,—the opening through which he had so often thrust the big oak logs to feed it. No one disturbed him; the heavy train went lumbering on and on, and he saw nothing at all of the beautiful mountains, and shining waters, and great forests through which he was being carried. He was hard at work getting through the straw and hay and twisted ropes; and at last he found the door of the stove, which he knew so well, and which was quite large enough for a child of his age to slip through. Slip through he did, as he had often done at home for fun, and curled himself up there to see if he could anyhow remain during many hours. He found that he could; air came in through the brass fret-work of the stove; and with admirable caution in such a little fellow, he leaned out, drew the hay and straw together, and rearranged the ropes, so that no one could ever have dreamed a little mouse had been at them. Then he curled himself up again, this time more like a dormouse than anything else; and, being safe inside his dear Hirschvogel and intensely cold, he went fast asleep as if he were in his own bed at home with Albrecht and Christof on either side of him. The train lumbered on, and the child slept soundly for a long while. When he did awake, it was quite dark; he could not see, and for a while he was sorely frightened, and sobbed in a quiet heart-broken fashion, thinking of them all at home. But August was brave, and he had a firm belief that God and Hirschvogel would take care of him. So he got over his terror and his sobbing both.

The goods-trains are usually very slow, and are many days doing what a quick train does in a few hours. This one was quicker than most, because it was bearing goods to the King of Bavaria; still, it took all the short winter's day and the long winter's night and half another day to go over ground that the mail-trains cover in a forenoon. It passed pretty Rosenheim, that marks the border of Bavaria. And here the Nuremberg stove, with August inside it, was lifted out heedfully and set under a covered way. When it was lifted out, the boy had hard work to keep in his screams; he was tossed to and fro as the men lifted the huge thing, and the earthenware walls of his beloved fire-king were not cushions of down. However, though they swore and grumbled at the weight of it, they never suspected that a living child was inside it, and they carried it out on to the platform and set it down under the roof of the goods-shed.  There it passed the rest of the night and all the next morning, and August was all the while within it.

He had still some of his loaf, and a little—a very little—of his sausage.  What he did begin to suffer was thirst.  It was many hours since he had last taken a drink from the wooden spout of their old pump, which brought them the sparkling, ice-cold water of the hills.  But, fortunately for him, the stove, having been marked and registered as "fragile and valuable," was not treated quite like a mere bale of goods, and the Rosenheim station-master resolved to send it on by a passenger-train that would leave there at daybreak.

Munich was reached, and August, hot and cold by turns, and shaking like a little aspen-leaf, felt himself once more carried out on the shoulders of men, rolled along on a truck, and finally set down, where he knew not, only he knew he was thirsty—so thirsty! If only he could have reached his hand out and scooped up a little snow!  He thought he had been moved on this truck many miles, but in truth the stove had been only taken from the railway-station to a shop in the Marienplatz.  Fortunately, the stove was always set upright on its four gilded feet, an injunction to that effect having been affixed to its written label, and on its gilded feet it stood now in the small dark curiosity-shop of one Hans Rhilfer.

"I shall not unpack it till Anton comes," he heard a man's voice say; and then he heard a key grate in a lock, and by the unbroken stillness that ensued he concluded he was alone, and ventured to peep through the straw and hay.  What he saw was a small square room filled with pots and pans, pictures, carvings, old blue jugs, old steel armor, shields, daggers, Chinese idols, Vienna china, Turkish rugs and all the rubbish of a *bric-a-brac* dealer's.  It seemed a wonderful place to him; but, oh! was there one drop of water in it all?  That was his single thought.  There

was not a drop of water, but there was a lattice window grated, and beyond the window was a wide stone ledge covered with snow. August cast one look at the locked door, darted out of his hiding-place, ran and opened the window, crammed the snow into his mouth again and again, and then flew back into the stove, drew the hay and straw over the place he entered by, and shut the brass door down on himself.

Presently the key turned in the lock, he heard heavy footsteps and the voice of the man who had said to his father, "You have a little mad dog; muzzle him!" The voice said, "Ay, ay, you have called me a fool many times. Now you shall see what I have gotten for two hundred dirty florins. *Potztausend!* never did *you* do such a stroke of work!"

Then the other voice grumbled and swore, and the steps of the two men approached more closely, and the heart of the child went pit-a-pat, pit-a-pat. They began to strip the stove of its wrappings; that he could tell by the noise they made with the hay and the straw. Soon they had stripped it wholly; that, too, he knew by the oaths and exclamations of wonder and surprise and rapture which broke from the man who had not seen it before.

"A right royal thing! A wonderful and never-to-be-rivalled thing! Sublime! magnificent! matchless!"

After standing by the Nuremberg master's work for nigh an hour, praising and marvelling, the men moved to a little distance and began talking of sums of money and divided profits, of which discourse he could make out no meaning. All he could make out was that the name of the king—the king—the king came very often in their arguments. He fancied at times they quarrelled, for they swore lustily and their voices rose hoarse and high; but after a while they seemed to agree to something, and were in great glee. He made out that they were going to show Hirschvogel to some great person. He kept quite still and dared not move.

Presently the door opened again sharply. He could hear the two dealers' voices murmuring unctuous words, in which "honor," "gratitude," and many fine long noble titles played the chief parts. The voice of another person, more clear and refined than theirs, answered them curtly, and then, close by the stove and the boy's ear, ejaculated a single "*Wunderschön!*"

The poor little boy, meanwhile, within, was hugged up into nothing, dreading that every moment the stranger would open the stove. And open it truly he did, and examined the brass-work of the door; but inside it was so dark that crouching August passed unnoticed, screwed up into a ball like a hedgehog as he was. The gentleman shut to the door at length, without having seen anything strange inside it; and then talked long and low with the tradesmen. The child could distinguish little that he said, except the name of the king and the word "gulden" again and again. After a while he went away, one of the dealers accompanying him, one of them lingering behind to bar up the shutters. Then this one also withdrew, double-locking the door.

# THE TREASURE CHEST

He would have to pass the night here, that was certain. He and Hirschvogel were locked in, but at least they were together. If only he could have had something to eat! He thought with a pang of how at this hour at home they ate the sweet soup, sometimes with apples in it from Aunt Maila's farm orchard, and sang together, and listened to Dorothea's reading of tales, and basked in the glow that beamed on them from the great Nuremberg fireking. After a time he dropped asleep.

Midnight was chiming from all the brazen tongues of the city when he awoke, and, all being still, ventured to put his head out the door of the stove to see why such a strange bright light was round him. What he saw was nothing less than all the *bric-a-brac* in motion.

A big jug was solemnly dancing a minuet with a plump Faenza jar; a tall Dutch clock was going through a gavotte with a spindle-legged ancient chair; an old violin of Cremona was playing itself; a queer shrill plaintive music that thought itself merry came from a painted spinnet covered with faded roses, and a Japanese bronze was riding along on a griffin. A great number of little Dresden cups and saucers were all skipping and waltzing; the teapots, with their broad round faces, were spinning their own lids like teetotums; and a little Saxe poodle, with a red ribbon at its throat, was running from one to another. August looked on at these mad freaks and felt no sensation of wonder. He only, as he heard the violin and the spinet playing, felt an irresistible desire to dance too. No doubt his face said what he wished; for a lovely little lady, all in pink and gold and white, with powdered hair, and high-heeled shoes, and all made of the very finest and fairest Meissen china, tripped up to him, and smiled, and gave him her hand, and led him out to a minuet.

"I am the Princess of Saxe-Royale," she said with a smile. Then he ventured to say to her: "Madame, my princess, could

you tell me kindly why some of the figures dance and speak, and some lie up in a corner like lumber? Is it rude to ask?"

"My dear child," said the powdered lady, "is it possible that you do not know the reason? Why, those silent, dull things are *imitation;* lies, falsehoods, fabrications! They only *pretend* to be what we *are!* They never wake up; how can they? No imitation ever had any soul in it yet."

Then from where the great stove stood there came a solemn voice. All eyes turned upon Hirschvogel, and the heart of its little human comrade gave a great jump of joy. At last he would hear Hirschvogel speak.

"My friends," said that clear voice from the turret of Nuremberg faience. "We were made in days when men were true creatures, and so we, the work of their hands, were true too. We derive all the value in us from the fact that our makers wrought at us with zeal, with integrity, with faith—not to win fortunes, but to do nobly an honest thing and create for the honor of the

Arts and God.  I see amidst you a little human thing who loves
me and in his own childish way loves Art.  Now I want him forever
to remember that we are what we are, and precious in the eyes of
the world, because centuries ago those who were of single mind
and of pure hand so created us, scorning sham and haste and
counterfeit.  Well do I recollect my master, Augustin Hirschvogel.
He led a wise and blameless life, and wrought in loyalty and love,
and made his time beautiful thereby.  For many, many years I,
once honored of emperors, dwelt in a humble house and warmed
in successive winters three generations of little, cold, hungry
children.  When I warmed them they forgot that they were hungry;
they laughed and told tales, and slept at last about my feet.  Then
I knew that, humble as had become my lot, it was one that my
master would have wished for me, and I was content.  That was
better than to stand in a great hall of a great city, cold and empty,
even though wise men came to gaze and throngs of fools gaped,
passing with flattering words.  Where I go now I know not; but
since I go from that humble house where they loved me, I shall be
sad and alone."

Then the voice sank away in silence, and a strange golden light
that had shone on the great stove faded away.  A soft pathetic
melody stole gently through the room.  It came from the old, old
spinet that was covered with the faded roses.

Then that sad, sighing music of a bygone day died too; the
clocks of the city struck six of the morning; day was rising over the
Bayerischerwald.  August awoke with a great start, and found
himself lying on the bare bricks of the floor of the chamber, and
all the *bric-a-brac* was lying quite still all around.

He rose slowly to his feet.  Tramp, tramp, came a heavy step
up the stair.  He had but a moment in which to scramble back
into the great stove, when the door opened and the two dealers
entered, bringing candles with them to see their way.

August was scarcely conscious of danger more than he was of cold or hunger, now that he had heard Hirschvogel speak. A marvelous sense of courage, of security, of happiness, was about him, like strong and gentle arms enfolding him and lifting him upwards—upwards—upwards! Hirschvogel would defend him.

The dealers undid the shutters, and then began to wrap up the stove once more in all its straw and hay and cordage. Presently they called up their porters, and the stove, heedfully swathed and tended as though it were some prince going on a journey, was borne on the shoulders of six stout Bavarians down the stairs and out of the door. Even behind all those wrappings August felt the icy bite of the intense cold at dawn of a winter's day in Munich. The men moved the stove with exceeding gentleness and care, so that he had often been far more roughly shaken in his big brothers' arms than he was in his journey now.

The stout carriers tramped right across Munich to the railway station. Whether for a long or a short journey, whether for weal or woe, the stove with August still within it, was once more hoisted up into a great van; but this time it was not all alone, and the two dealers as well as the six porters were all with it.

Though the men grumbled about the state of the roads and the season, they were hilarious and well content, for they laughed often, and August, like a shrewd little boy as he was, thought to himself, with a terrible pang: "They have sold Hirschvogel for some great sum! They have sold him already!"

It is but an hour and a quarter that the train usually takes to pass from Munich to the Wurm-See or Lake of Starnberg; but this morning the journey was much slower, because the way was encumbered by snow. When it did reach Possenhofen and stop, and the stove was lifted out once more, August could see through the fretwork of the brass door that this Wurm-See was a calm and noble piece of water, with low wooded banks and distant mountains,

a peaceful, serene place, full of rest. Before he had time to get more than a glimpse of the green gliding surface, the stove was again lifted up and placed on a large boat that was in waiting. The boat then moved across the lake to Leoni.

Presently they touched the pier at Leoni.

"Now, men, for a stout mile and half!" said one of the dealers to his porters, who, stout, strong men as they were, showed a disposition to grumble at their task. Encouraged by large promises, they shouldered sullenly the Nuremberg stove, grumbling again at its preposterous weight, but little dreaming that they carried within it a small, panting, trembling boy.

The way the men took was a mile and a half in length, but the road was heavy with snow, and the burden they bore was heavier still. The dealers cheered them on, swore at them and praised them in one breath. The road seemed terribly long to the anxious tradesmen, to the plodding porters, to the poor little man inside the stove, as he kept sinking and rising, sinking and rising, with each of their steps.

Where they were going he had no idea, only after a very long time he lost the sense of the fresh icy wind blowing on his face through the brass-work above, and felt by their movements beneath him that they were mounting steps or stairs. Then he heard a great many different voices, but he could not understand what was being said. He felt that his bearers paused some time, then moved on and on again. Their feet went so softly he thought they must be moving on carpet, and as he felt a warm air come to him, he concluded that he was in some heated chambers. What he fancied was that he was in some museum, like that which he had seen in the city of Innsbruck.

The voices he heard were very hushed, and the steps seemed to go away, far away, leaving him alone with Hirschvogel. He dared not look out, but he peeped through the brass-work, and all he could see was a big carved lion's head in ivory, with a gold crown atop. It belonged to a velvet fauteuil, but he could not see the chair, only the ivory lion. There was a delicious fragrance in the air,—a fragrance as of flowers. "Only how can it be flowers?" thought August. "It is November!" From afar off, as it seemed, there came dreamy, exquisite music.

He did not know it, but he was in the royal castle of Berg, and the music he heard was the music of Wagner, who was playing in a distant room.

Presently he heard a fresh step near him, and he heard a low voice say, close behind him, "So!" An exclamation, no doubt, of admiration and wonder at the beauty of Hirschvogel. Then the same voice said, after a long pause, during which, as August thought, this new-comer was examining all the details of the wondrous fire-tower, "It was well bought; it is exceedingly beautiful! It is undoubtedly the work of Augustin Hirschvogel."

Then the hand of the speaker turned the round handle of the brass door, and the fainting soul of the poor little prisoner within grew sick with fear. The door was slowly drawn open, some one bent down and looked in, and the same voice called aloud, in surprise, "What is this in it? A live child!"

Then August, terrified beyond all self-control, and dominated by one master-passion, sprang out of the body of the stove and fell at the feet of the speaker.

"Oh, let me stay! Pray, meinherr, let me stay!" he sobbed. "I have come all the way with Hirschvogel!"

Some gentlemen's hands seized him, not gently by any means, and their lips angrily muttered in his ear, "Little knave, peace! be quiet! hold your tongue! It is the king!"

They were about to drag him out of the august atmosphere as if he had been some dangerous beast come there to slay, but the voice he had heard said in kind accents, "Poor child! he is very young. Let him go. Let him speak to me."

The word of a king is law to his courtiers; so, sorely against their wish, the angry and astonished chamberlains let August slide out of their grasp, and he stood there in his little rough sheepskin coat and his thick, mud-covered boots, with his curling hair all in a tangle, in the midst of the most beautiful chamber he had ever dreamed of, and in the presence of a young man with a beautiful dark face, and eyes full of dreams and fire; and the young man said to him,—

"My child, how came you here, hidden in this stove? Be not afraid, tell me the truth. I am the king."

August in an instinct of homage cast his great battered black hat with the tarnished gold tassels down on the floor of the room, and folded his little brown hands in supplication. He was too intensely in earnest to be in any way abashed; he was too lifted out of himself by his love for Hirschvogel to be conscious of any awe before any earthly majesty. He was only so glad—so glad it was the king.

"Oh, dear king!" he said, with trembling entreaty in his voice, "Hirschvogel was ours. We have loved it all our lives; and father sold it. When I saw that it did really go from us, then I said to myself I would go with it; and I have come all the way inside it. And last night it spoke and said beautiful things. And I pray you to let me live with it. I will go out every morning and cut wood for it and you, if only you will let me stay beside it. No one ever has fed it with fuel but me since I grew big enough, and it loves me;— it does indeed; it said so last night; and it said that it had been happier with us than if it were in any palace—"

And then his breath failed him, and, as he lifted his eager, pale face to the king's, great tears were falling down his cheeks.

Now, the king liked all poetic and uncommon things, and there was that in the child's face which pleased and touched him. He motioned to his gentlemen to leave the little boy alone.

"What is your name?" he asked him.

"I am August Strehla. My father is Karl Strehla. We live in Hall; and Hirschvogel has been ours so long,—so long!"

His lips quivered with a broken sob.

"And have you truly traveled in this stove all the way from Tyrol?"

"Yes," said August, "no one thought to look inside till you did."

The king laughed; then another view of the matter occurred to him. "Who bought the stove of your father?" he inquired.

"Traders of Munich," said August.

"What sum did they pay, do you know?"

"Two hundred florins," said August, with a great sigh of shame. "It was so much money, and he is so poor, and there are so many of us."

The king turned to his gentlemen-in-waiting. "Did these dealers of Munich come with the stove?"

He was answered in the affirmative. He desired them to be

sought for and brought before him. As one of his chamberlains hastened on the errand, the monarch looked at August with compassion.

"You are very pale, little fellow; when did you eat last?"

"I had some bread and sausage with me; yesterday afternoon I finished it."

"You would like to eat now?"

"If I might have a little water I would be glad; my throat is very dry."

The king had water and wine brought for him, and cake also;

but August, though he drank eagerly, could not swallow anything. His mind was in too great a tumult.

"May I stay with Hirschvogel?" he said, with feverish agitation.

"Wait a little," said the king, and asked, abruptly, "what do you wish to be when you are a man?"

"A painter. I wish to be what Hirschvogel was,—I mean the master that made *my* Hirschvogel."

"I understand," said the king.

Then the two dealers were brought into their sovereign's presence. They were so terribly alarmed, not being either so innocent or so ignorant as August was, that they were trembling as though they were being led to the slaughter, and they were so utterly astonished too at a child having come all the way from Tyrol in the stove, as a gentleman of the court had just told them this child had done, that they could not tell what to say or where to look, and presented a very foolish aspect indeed.

"Did you buy this stove of this boy's father for two hundred florins?" the king asked; and his voice was no longer soft and kind as it had been when addressing the child, but very stern.

"Yes, your majesty," murmured the trembling traders.

"And how much did the gentleman who purchased it for me give to you?"

"Two thousand ducats, your majesty," muttered the dealers, frightened out of their wits, and telling the truth in their fright.

"You will give at once to this boy's father the two thousand gold ducats that you received, less the two hundred Austrian florins that you paid him," said the king. "You are great rogues. Be thankful you are not more greatly punished."

He dismissed them by a sign to his courtiers.

August heard, and felt dazzled yet miserable. Two thousand gold Bavarian ducats for his father! Why, his father would never need to go any more to the salt-baking! And yet, whether for ducats or for florins, Hirschvogel was sold just the same, and would the king let him stay with it?—would he?

"Oh, do! please do!" he murmured, joining his little brown weather-stained hands, and kneeling before the young monarch.

He looked down on the child and smiled once more.

"Rise up, my little man," he said, in a kind voice; "kneel only to your God. Will I let you stay with your Hirschvogel? Yes, I will; you shall stay at my court, and you shall be taught to be a painter. You must grow up worthily, and win all the laurels at our Schools of Art, and if when you are twenty-one years old you have done well and bravely, then I will give you your Nuremberg stove. And now go away with this gentleman, and be not afraid, and you shall light a fire every morning in Hirschvogel, but you will not need to go out and cut the wood."

Then he smiled and stretched out his hand; the courtiers tried to make August understand that he ought to bow and touch it with his lips, but August could not understand that anyhow; he was too happy. He threw his two arms about the king's knees, and kissed his feet passionately.

August is only a scholar yet, but he is a happy scholar, and promises to be a great man. Sometimes he goes back for a few days to Hall, where the gold ducats have made his father prosperous. In the old house-room there is a large white porcelain stove of Munich, the king's gift to Dorothea and 'Gilda.

And August never goes home without going into the great church and saying his thanks to God, who blessed his strange winter's journey in the Nuremberg stove. As for his dream in the dealers' room that night, he will never admit that he did dream it; he still declares that he saw it all, and heard the voice of Hirschvogel. And who shall say that he did not, for what is the gift of the poet and the artist except to see the sights which others cannot see and hear the sounds that others cannot hear?

*—Abridged*

### A CAVALIER TUNE
*Boot and Saddle*
#### ROBERT BROWNING

Boot, saddle, to horse, and away!
Rescue my castle before the hot day
Brightens to blue from its silvery gray!
*Boot, saddle, to horse, and away!*

Ride past the suburbs, asleep as you'd say;
Many's the friend there, will listen and pray
"God's luck to gallants that strike up the lay—
*Boot, saddle, to horse, and away!*"

Forty miles off, like a roebuck at bay,
Flouts Castle Brancepeth the Roundheads array!
Who laughs, "Good fellows ere this, by my fay,
*Boot, saddle, to horse, and away!*"

Who? My wife Gertrude; that, honest and gay,
Laughs when you talk of surrendering, "Nay!
I've better counsellors; what counsel they?
*Boot, saddle, to horse, and away!*"

## The Secret Door

### Susan Coolidge

Knowle, in Kent, is an ancient manor-house. It stands knee-deep in rich garden and pasture lands, with hay-fields and apple-orchards stretching beyond, and solemn oak woods which whisper and shake their wise heads when the wind blows, as though possessed of secrets which must not be spoken.

Very much as it looks today, it looked two hundred and thirty years ago, when Charles the First was king of England. Blue Christmas smokes curled from the twisted chimneys in 1645, just as they will this year and the same dinnery fragrance filled the air. A few changes there may be—thicker trees, beds of gay flowers which were not known in that day; and where once the moat—a ditch-like stream of green water covered with weeds and scum—ran round the walls, is now a trimly cut border of verdant turf. But in all important respects the house keeps its old look, undisturbed by modern times and ways.

In the same nursery where modern boys and girls eat, sleep, and learn their A, B, C to-day, two children lived—little Ralph Tresham and his sister Henrietta. Quaint, old-fashioned creatures they would look to us now; but, in spite of their formal dresses and speech, they were bright and merry and happy as any children you can find among your acquaintances. Ralph's name was pronounced "Rafe," and he called his sister "Hexie."

Christmas did not come to Knowle in its usual bright shape in 1645. Gloom and sadness and anxiety overshadowed the house; and though the little ones did not understand what the cause of the anxiety was, they felt something wrong, and went about quietly whispering to each other in corners, instead of whooping and laughing, as had been their wont. They had eaten their Christmas beef, and toasted the king in a thimbleful of wine, as usual, but their mother cried when they did so; and Joyce, the old butler, had carried off the pudding with a face like a funeral. So after dinner they crept away to the nursery, and there, by the window, began a long whispered talk. Hexie had something very exciting to tell.

"Nurse thought I was asleep," she said, "but I wasn't quite; and when they began to talk I woke up. Did you know that there were such creatures as Bogies, Rafe? Dorothy thinks we have got one in our house, and that its hole is in the great gallery, because once when she was there dusting the armor, she heard a queer noise in the wall, and what else could it be? It eats a great deal, does the Bogie. That's the reason nurse is sure we have got one. It ate all the cold sheep's-head yesterday, and the day before half the big pasty. No victual is safe in the larder, the Bogie has such a big appetite, nurse says."

"I remember about the sheep's-head," said Rafe, meditatively. "Almost all of it was left, and I looked to see it come in cold; but when I asked, Joyce said there was none. Cold sheep's-head is very good. Do you remember how much Humphrey used to like it?"

"I don't remember exactly, it is so long ago," replied Hexie. "How long is it since brother Humphrey went away? Won't he ever come back?"

"I asked Winifred once, but she only said God knew, that nothing had been heard of him since the battle when the Roundheads took the king prisoner. He might be dead, or he might be escaped into foreign parts—and then she cried, oh, so hard, Hexie! But, about the Bogie, how curious it must be to meet one! Oh, I say, let us go to the gallery now, and listen if we can hear any strange noises there. Will you?"

"Oh, Rafe! I'm afraid. I don't quite like—"

"But you can't be afraid if I'm there," said Rafe, valiantly; "besides, I'll put on Humphrey's old sword which he left behind. Then if the Bogie comes—we shall see!"

Rafe spoke like a conquering hero, Hexie thought; so, though she trembled, she made no further objection, but stood by while he lifted down the sword, helped to fasten its belt over his shoulder, and followed along the passageway which led to the gallery. The heavy sword clattered and rattled as it dragged on the floor, and the sound was echoed in a ghostly way, which renewed Hexie's fears.

"Rafe! Rafe! let us go back," she cried.

"Go back yourself if you are afraid," replied Ralph, stoutly; and as going back alone through the dim passage seemed just then worse than staying where she was, Hexie stayed.

Very softly they unlatched the gallery door, and stole in. It was a long, lofty apartment, panelled with cedar-wood, to which time had given a beautiful light brown color. The ceiling, of the same wood, was carved here and there, with shields, coats of arms, and other devices. There was little furniture; one tall cabinet, a few high-backed Dutch chairs, and some portraits hanging on the walls. The sun, not yet quite set, poured a stream of red light across the polished floor, leaving the far corners and the empty spaces formidably dusk. The children had seldom been in the gallery at this hour, and it looked to them almost like a strange place, not at all as it did at noon-day when they came to jump up and down the slippery floor, and play hide-and-seek in the corners which now seemed so dark and dismal.

Even Rafe felt the difference, and shivered in spite of his bold heart and the big sword by his side. Timidly they went forward, hushing their footsteps and peering furtively into the shadows. Suddenly Hexie stopped with a little scream.

Close to them stood a huge suit of armor, larger and taller than a man. The empty eye-holes of the helmet glared out quite like real eyes, and the whole figure was terrible enough to frighten any little girl. But it was not at the armor that Hexie screamed; the iron man was an old friend of the children's. Many a game of hide-and-seek had they played around, and behind, and even inside him; for Humphrey had contrived a cunning way by which the figure could be taken to pieces and put together again; and more than once Rafe had been popped inside, and had lain shaking with laughter while Hexie vainly searched for him through all the gallery. This had not happened lately, for Rafe was hardly strong enough to manage by himself the screws and hinges which opened the armor; but he knew the iron man too well to scream at him, and so did Hexie. The object which excited her terror was something different, and so strange and surprising that it is no wonder she screamed.

Close by the armor, half hidden by a curtain of heavy tapestry, was an open door, where never door had been known to be. It stood ajar, and dimly visible inside was a narrow staircase winding upward.

"The hole of the Bogie!" gasped Hexie, clutching at Rafe's arm. He started, and felt for the sword. It rattled fearfully, and the sound completed Hexie's terror. She burst away, flew like a scared lapwing down the gallery, along the passages, and never stopped till she reached the nursery and her own bed, where, with two pillows and the quilt drawn over her head, she

# THE TREASURE CHEST

lay sobbing bitterly at the thought of Ralph left behind, to be eaten perhaps by the Bogie! Poor little Hexie!

Ralph, meanwhile, stood his ground. His heart beat very fast, but he would not run away,—that was for girls. It must be owned, however, that when a moment later the sound of muffled voices became audible down the stairs, he trembled extremely, and was guilty of hiding behind the curtain.

The voices drew nearer, steps sounded, and two figures came out of the narrow doorway. Could there be two Bogies? No wonder they ate so much. But in another minute all thought of Bogies vanished from Ralph's mind, for in one of the figures he recognized his own sister Winifred.

Her companion was a man. There was something familiar in his form. It moved forward, and Ralph jumped so that the big sword rattled again. Bogie number two was his brother Humphrey, mourned as dead ever since the summer before, when so many brave gentlemen gave up their lives for King Charles at the battle of Naseby.

"What noise was that?" whispered Winifred, fearfully.

"Some sound from below," replied Humphrey, after listening a moment. "Must you go, Winnie?"

"I must, dear Humphrey. I dare not absent myself longer lest I be missed and suspected. Oh, if tomorrow were but over, and you safe on the French lugger and over the sea! I cannot breathe while this hiding goes on, and you ever in danger of being discovered and taken by the Roundheads."

"I suppose I ought to be glad also," said Humphrey, ruefully, "but to me that French lugger means exile, and loneliness for the rest of my life, perhaps. Better have laid down my life with the rest at Naseby, in striking one last blow for the king."

"Don't, don't speak so!" protested Winifred, tearfully. "You are alive, thank God; and once these wars are over we may rejoin you, and have a happy home somewhere, if not in the land of our fathers. Now, dear Humphrey, have you all you need for the night?"

"Christmas cheer," said Humphrey, in a would-be cheerful voice. "Beef and ale,—what better fare could be? You are a gallant provider, my Winnie. That sheep's-head was wondrous savory. I say though, what do the servants think of the famine I create in the larder?"

"Oh, the stupid things fancy that a Bogie has taken up his residence here. A very hungry Bogie, Joyce calls the creature!"

The brother and sister laughed; then they kissed each other.

"Good-night, Winifred."

"Good-night, brother." And Humphrey vanished up the stairs. Winifred lingered a moment; then, as if remembering something, opened the door again and ran after him. Ralph marked that she laid her hand on a particular boss in the carved wainscot, and pressed it in hard, whereon the door sprang open. He stole out, laid his hand on the same boss, and felt the spring give way under his touch. Some undefined idea of stealing in later, to make Humphrey a visit, was in his head; but he heard Winifred returning, and hurried out of the gallery. Putting back the sword in its place, he entered the nursery. No Hexie was visible, but a sobbing sound drew his attention to a tumbled heap on the bed.

"Is that you, Hexie? Why, what are you crying about?" pulling away the pillow, which she held tight.

"Oh, Rafe! Then the Bogie didn't eat you after all!" And Hexie buried her tear-stained face in his shoulder.

"Bogie! Nonsense! There are no such things as Bogies!"

"What was it, then, that lived up that dreadful stairs?"

"I can't tell you; only it was nothing at all dreadful. And, Hexie, don't say a word about that door to any one, will you? It might make great trouble if you did."

"I did tell Deborah, when she fetched the candle and asked why I cried, that I saw a strange door in the gallery," faltered Hexie, truthful, though penitent.

"Oh! Hexie, how could you? I don't like Deborah, her father is a crop-eared knave and a Roundhead. Humphrey said so one day. How could you talk to her about the door, Hexie?"

"I—don't know. I was frightened, and she asked me," sobbed Hexie. "Will it do any harm, Rafe?"

"It may," said Rafe, gloomily. "But don't cry, Hexie. You meant no harm, at all events."

"Oh, don't speak so gravely and so like Joyce," said Hexie, much troubled. She cried herself to sleep that night. Deborah, who undressed her, asked many questions about the gallery and the door.

"It was very dark, and perhaps I mistook,"—that was all Hexie could be made to say. Ralph was disturbed and wakeful, and slept later than usual next morning. He jumped up in a hurry and made what haste he could with dressing and breakfast, but it seemed as though they never took so much time before; and all the while he ate he was conscious of a stir and bustle in the house, which excited his curiosity very much. Knocking— the sound of feet—something unusual going on.

As soon as possible he slipped away from the nurse and ran to the gallery. The door was half open. He looked in, and stood still with terror. Men in brown uniforms and steel caps were there sounding the walls and tapping the floor-boards with staves —Roundheads in search of Humphrey! The gallery seemed full of them, though when Rafe counted there were but five.

# THE TREASURE CHEST

"This man of iron was, in all likelihood, a Malignant also," he heard one of them say, striking the armor with his fist.

"He is somewhat old for that. Methinks that is armor of the time of that man of blood, Harry the Eighth. Move it aside, Jothan, that we may search the farther panel."

So the heavy figure was thrust into a corner, and the men went on tapping with their wands. Rafe groaned within himself when he heard them declare that the wall sounded hollow, and saw them searching for a spring. Twenty times it seemed as though they must have lighted on the right place. Twenty times they just missed it.

"We were ill advised to come without tools," declared the man who seemed leader of the party. "Come thou to my shop, Peter Kettle, and thou, Bartimeus and Zerubbabel, and we will fetch such things as are needful. Jotham, stay thou here, to see that no man escapeth from the concealment behind the wall."

So four of the men went away, leaving Jotham striding up and down as on guard. Presently came a shout from beneath the window,—

"Jotham! our leader hath dropped his pouch in which are the keys of the smithy. Hasten and bring it to the outer door."

"Aye, aye!" answered Jotham, and, pouch in hand, he ran down the stairs. Now was Rafe's opportunity. Like a flash he was across the gallery, his hand on the boss. The door flew open, and he fell into the arms of Humphrey, who, sword in hand and teeth set, stood on the lower step of the staircase, prepared to sell his liberty as dearly as possible.

"Rafe! little Rafe!" he exclaimed.

"Hush! The man will come back," panted Rafe. "Come away—hide—oh, where?" Then with a sudden inspiration he dragged his brother toward the iron man. "Get inside," he cried. "They will never think of searching there! Oh, Humphrey —make haste! Get inside!"

There was no time to be lost. With the speed of desperation, Humphrey unscrewed, lifted, stepped inside the armor. Rafe slipped the fastenings together, whispering, "Shut your eyes," and flew back to his hiding-place. Just in time, for Jotham's step was on the stair, and next moment he entered the gallery, and resumed his march up and down, little dreaming that the man sought for was peeping through the helmet holes at him, not three feet away.

Presently the other soldiers came back with hammers and wrenches, and in a short time the beautiful wainscot, split into pieces, lay on the floor. Suddenly there was a shout. The secret door had flown open, and the staircase stood revealed. Four of the men, with pikes and pistols, prepared to ascend, while the fifth guarded the opening below.

At that moment Winifred entered the gallery from the farther end. She turned deadly pale when she saw the open door.

"Oh! Heaven have mercy!" she cried, and dropped half fainting into a chair.

Rafe darted across the floor and seized her hand.

"Hush," he whispered. "Don't say a word, sister. *He* is safe."

"He? Who?" cried the amazed Winifred.

But now voices sounded from above. The men were coming down. Winifred rallied her courage, rose, and went forward.

She was still very white, but she spoke in a steady voice.

# THE TREASURE CHEST

Her two brothers, Humphrey in his hiding-place and little Rafe by her side, both admired her greatly.

"What is the meaning of this, Jotham Green?" she demanded. "By what warrant do you enter and spoil our house?"

"By the warrant which all true men have to search for traitors," said Jotham.

"You will find none such here," responded Winifred, firmly.

"We find the lurking-place in which one such has doubtless lain," said Zerubbabel. "Where holes exist, look out for vermin."

"You are less than civil, neighbor. An old house like this has many strange nooks and corners of which the inhabitants may have neither use nor knowledge. If your search is done, I will beg you to make good the damage you have caused as best you may, and with as little noise as possible, that my mother be not alarmed. Jotham Green, you are a good workman, I know. I recollect how deftly you once repaired that cabinet for us."

All the men knew Winifred, and her calm and decided manner made its impression. Jotham slowly picked up the fragments of the panelling and began to fit them together. The rest consulted, and at last rather sheepishly, and with a muttered half apology about "wrong information," went away, taking with them the injured woodwork, which Jotham undertook to repair. Rafe's first words after they disappeared were,—

"Winifred, you must dismiss Deborah. It is she that has betrayed us."

"How do you know that, Rafe?"

Then it all came out. Winifred listened to the tale with streaming tears.

"Oh, Rafe, my darling, how brave you were! You played the man for us today, and have saved Humphrey. The men will not return today, and tonight the lugger sails."

And Humphrey was saved. Before morning, well disguised,

he had made his way across country to a little fishing-port, embarked, and reached France without further accident.

So that strange Christmas adventure ended happily. It was all long, long ago. But still the beautiful old manor-house stands amid its gardens and pasture lands, with the silvery look of time on its gray walls. Still the armed figure keeps guard beside the secret staircase, the tapestry hangs in the old heavy folds, evening reddens the cedar walls and the polished floor, and everything occupies the same place and wears the same look that it did when little Rafe played the man in that gallery, and saved his brother Humphrey, more than two hundred years ago.

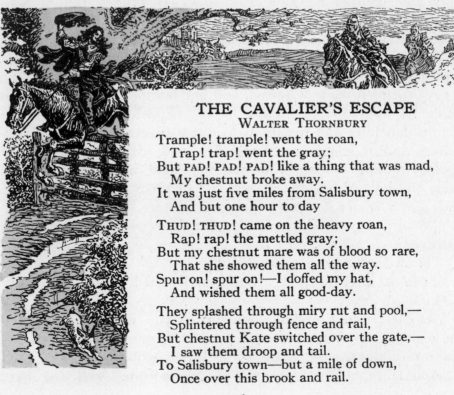

## THE CAVALIER'S ESCAPE
### WALTER THORNBURY

Trample! trample! went the roan,
   Trap! trap! went the gray;
But PAD! PAD! PAD! like a thing that was mad,
   My chestnut broke away.
It was just five miles from Salisbury town,
   And but one hour to day

THUD! THUD! came on the heavy roan,
   Rap! rap! the mettled gray;
But my chestnut mare was of blood so rare,
   That she showed them all the way.
Spur on! spur on!—I doffed my hat,
   And wished them all good-day.

They splashed through miry rut and pool,—
   Splintered through fence and rail,
But chestnut Kate switched over the gate,—
   I saw them droop and tail.
To Salisbury town—but a mile of down,
   Once over this brook and rail.

# THE TREASURE CHEST

Trap! Trap! I heard their echoing hoofs
    Past the walls of mossy stone,
The roan flew on at a staggering pace,
    But blood is better than bone.
I patted old Kate, and gave her the spur,
    For I knew it was all my own.

But trample! trample! came their steeds,
    And I saw their wolf's eyes burn,
I felt like a royal hart at bay,
    And made me ready to turn.
I looked where highest grew the May,
    And deepest arched the fern.

I flew at the first knave's sallow throat,
    One blow, and he was down.
The second rogue fired twice, and missed,
    I sliced the villain's crown,—
Clove through the rest—and flogged brave Kate,
    *Fast, fast to Salisbury town!*

Pad! pad! they came on the level sward,
    Thud! thud! upon the sand,—
With a gleam of swords and a burning match,
    And a shaking of flag and hand;
But one long bound, and I passed the gate,
    Safe from the canting band.

DONN P. CRANE

## The Adventures of Alexander Selkirk

*Being a true Account of one Mr. Alexander Selkirk, Master of a Merchant-Man who was left ashore on a desolate Island in the South-Seas, where he lived Four Years and Four Months without seeing the Face of Man. To which is added a Description of the Island where he was cast; how he subsisted; the several Strange Things he saw; and how he used to spend his Time. Told from the Accounts of Captain Woodes Rogers, Sir Richard Steele and other Eminent Men, who had the Tale directly from the Lips of the said Alexander Selkirk in Person, he being further known to Fame by reason of his Adventures having furnished to Daniel Defoe the idea for writing of Robinson Crusoe.*

IN the year 1704, there was cruising off the coast of Mexico an English galley, by name the Cinque Ports, 96 tons burden, 16 guns, and sixty odd men. The Cinque Ports had been a twelvemonth or more in those parts, at first in company with another vessel under Captain Dampier, on a voyage of exploration and adventure. In those days the greed of France and Spain to rule the world and crowd England out of the South Seas, made the relations of England with those countries none of the friendliest, and the British government commissioned private vessels to make war on the boats of the enemy wherever they might overtake them on the high seas. Of such sort was the Cinque Ports, and she had sailed along the rich gold coast of Spanish America, now and again running down some Spanish galleon, and meeting with sundry and divers adventures. Her commander was one Captain Straddling, a cross-grained, quarrelsome fellow, and he had serving under him as sailing master of the vessel, a certain hot-headed, independent young Scotchman, by name Alexander Selkirk, or Selcraig, as it is more properly written, son of a well-to-do tanner and shoemaker of Largo in Fifeshire, and a follower of the sea from his youth. Now Selkirk was an expert and able seaman, but from the start of the voyage he got on none too well with

Straddling. Straddling was an insolent bully. Right and left it was hot tongue and heavy fist wherever Straddling appeared on deck. Month after month, Selkirk held his temper in check— Straddling was his superior officer and he had a sailor's wish and training to obey. Yet was he one to brook domineering from no man, and now and again when Straddling rode his high horse, there was an outburst from Selkirk that threatened the gathering of a terrific storm.

As they sailed day after day and month after month, the Cinque Ports grew leaky and altogether unseaworthy, so Captain Straddling found himself forced at last to put in for fresh water and repairs at the island of Juan Fernandez, some four hundred miles off the coast of Chili. Juan Fernandez was lonely, wild and uninhabited. It was off the beaten track of commerce and was rarely visited by vessels of any kind, but Straddling had been forced earlier on the same voyage to put in there, and thither under stress of necessity he went again. During the three weeks or so that they lay to in the chief bay of the island, the differences between Straddling and Selkirk grew daily worse, till at last on the very day when the vessel was getting under way, an angry discussion arose. Hotter and hotter it grew. It is not improbable that fists as well as tongues came into play to settle the question, but, however that may be, the upshot of the whole matter was that Selkirk's temper took such furious fire, he burst out the door of the Captain's cabin and rushed up the companionway, shouting:

"Let me off this crazy vessel! Put me ashore, I say! I'll sail not a day longer under such an obstinate, pig-headed mule!"

The Captain followed his irate master onto the deck, bestowing upon him a string of like forceful compliments and bawling out:

"Down with the pinnace! Take him ashore! Off with the mutinous hound! He's turned out o' service!"

While the sailors swarmed to the small boat, Selkirk calmed

himself sufficiently to gather together certain of his belongings, and, having piled these into the pinnace, he was over the side of the galley and being rowed off to the shore almost before he knew it.

He saw before him a wild, luxuriant and yet savage coast, a mass of jagged, volcanic rock, hurled up in ages agone by some mighty disturbance of the earth and rudely piled into blocks and pinnacles.   Mountains towered above, and over all rose the craggy peak of El Yunque (the Anvil) of which no man knew whether or no it would one day belch forth fire and overwhelm all that lay at its base with a mighty stream of lava.   Yet Selkirk's spirit, at that moment, was as wild and untamed as that savage shore, and the fire within him smouldering, ready to flame, like volcanic fires of the earth.   To such a state of mind the shore was inviting rather than forbidding.   Anger and defiance buoyed him up.   He held his head high and his eyes were glowing.   Straddling himself had command of the small boat, and the moment its keel grated on the sand, Selkirk sprang lightly ashore, standing by with the utmost unconcern while the Captain gave orders concerning the unloading of his luggage.

The matter was carried through with the greatest dispatch and the sailors were soon bidding their comrade a sorrowful farewell, while Straddling sat in the boat and in surly fashion called them to make haste and be off.

All at once—Selkirk never knew how it came about so quickly, —out there, bobbing up and down on the swelling blue, half way back to the galley and going at a tremendous clip, he saw the small boat, loaded with men, and there alone on the shore he stood, Alexander Selkirk, alone, all alone!

In a trice with a sudden revulsion of feeling, it came over him what he had done.   Anger and defiance were dead.   The scales had fallen from his eyes.   He knew what he had done.   To stay alone on a savage shore—to hear no human voice—to see no

human face—for years, perhaps forever! He raised his voice in a cry that was almost a shriek, stretched out his arms toward his comrades and rushed to the very edge of the water.

"Come back! Come back! Come back!" he cried. The wind carried his voice away, and yet it seemed to him he heard from the stern of the pinnace where the Captain sat, a sound of mocking laughter. Even while it echoed in his ears, the men in the small boat boarded the larger vessel. All sail was set, and the Cinque Ports made off out of the bay and into the Pacific. He watched with straining eyes till her sails, a mere speck in the distance, dipped down behind the horizon, and the whole vast blue of ocean was left stretching empty and lone before him.

How long he stood there, almost in a stupor staring off to sea, he never knew, but suddenly he became aware that the stillness about him was so intense, it seemed of a truth to shriek in his ears. Thus brought back to himself, he looked about and observed that the sun was low in the sky. In a short time darkness would swoop down upon his solitude. Now he had no knowledge whether or no savage beasts abounded on the island, and he judged it to be most necessary that he find a shelter ere nightfall. Accordingly, though with weak and trembling knees, he searched along the shore. In a little ravine at no great distance back from the beach, he came upon a cave of moderate dimensions that offered a most excellent retreat and lay not far from a stream of fresh water.

Hither he dragged his belongings from the place on the sand where they had been dumped, and being now at liberty and of a mind to take stock of the same, he found he had with him a sea chest containing his bedding and a few extra articles of clothing, a firelock, a pound of gunpowder, a large quantity of bullets, a few pounds of tobacco, a hatchet, a knife, a kettle, a Bible, several books that concerned navigation, and his mathematical instruments. In provisions for the sustenance of life, he had but the quantity of two meals. It being then nearly dark, and no opportunity offering to search for food that night, he was obliged for the present to appease his hunger by consuming a share from his slender store. He then closed the entrance to his cave by means of his sea chest and laid himself down to sleep with his firelock close by his side. Several times during the night he fancied he heard growling and roaring as of wild beasts, but the darkness passed without incident and the sun rose with remarkable splendor.

It was early October, being spring in that latitude, and within the verdant little gorge where the cave was situated, all was bud and bloom and twitter of birds and gladsome play of sunlight and shadows. Selkirk, notwithstanding, had eyes for none of the beauties about him. He thought only of the misfortune, swift and terrible, that was come upon him. For days he sat moping and brooding by the sea shore, straining his eyes to catch sight of a sail. Not till the darkness of night made it impossible longer to watch, did he close his eyes, and then he slept but poorly. As to eating, he never ate anything at all till the extreme of hunger constrained him, and even then he took no care to make his victuals palatable. He ate only of the craw-fish and turtle to be found on the shore, for he felt spell-bound to the beach. Fortunately he had with him a kettle, and by patient trial he learned to get fire by rubbing two sticks together on his knees, after the Indian fashion. Sometimes he broiled the shell-fish and sometimes he boiled them, but he found nothing that he ate to his taste for want of salt to season it.

The whole island was in truth rich in natural beauties, in hills and valleys, delightful springs and leaping mountain streams, but Selkirk saw no beauty in it anywhere. To him its loneliness, its deadly stillness, made it all as frightful as some distorted vision of a dream. He only left the shore to climb up to a certain high point by the side of El Yunque, whence a gap in the trap-rock offered a still wider view of the sea. He made no count of days, he took no care of himself, of his clothing, or the cave in which he lived. All his soul was absorbed in that one thought, to watch for a sail, and he wore a beaten track from the shore to his look-out, from his look-out to the shore.

Along in November, as he slept an uneasy sleep within his cave, he was suddenly awakened by the increase of that growling and roaring as of wild beasts which had disturbed his first night on the island. It sounded somewhat between the howling of wolves and the thunderous roar of larger beasts and was of a nearness to make him hold all night, close by, his firelock. He never closed his eyes again for uncertainty but when the sun was risen and he stepped cautiously out of his cave towards the shore, there before him on the beach he saw myriads of seals that had come up out of the sea during the night. Some were in the water but more were on the land and these were moving their heads about, raising themselves on their flippers, roaring and bellowing. It being Selkirk's custom at once to go to his look-out on the beach, he approached the seals with some uncertainty as to their temper in letting him pass through. He held his firelock ready to beat them off with the butt in case they made at him, but he found them so surly and determined not to give way, that he was forced to beat a retreat before them. In a short time their numbers had so increased as others drew up out of the sea that they lined

the shore very thick for above half a mile of ground all around the bay. It appeared this was the spot where it was their custom to come each year and raise their young, and though seals be usually peaceable creatures, as there came to be many young among them, the old ones grew still more surly. Far from moving out of the way, they would rise up on their flippers in their desire to protect the whelps and make at a man fiercely like an angry dog, if he offered to go among them. Moreover, day and night, they kept up a continuous noise of a hideous sort. So Selkirk was obliged to avoid the beach and largely to keep his look-out from the high place on the side of El Yunque, and in his present state of mind the dreadful howlings and voices of these monsters of the deep seemed almost too terrible to be borne. He had been in the past not of a nature to bear misfortune calmly, and many a time from sheer impatience and impotent inward rage against the helplessness of his wretched lot he shook his fists and cried aloud; and as no sail appeared day after day, he even meditated casting himself into the sea. "Could the thought of man," he often demanded of himself, "devise a more utterly miserable lot than life alone on a desert isle?"

And then at last one day as he was going through his sea chest in search of some trifle or other, his hand fell upon the Bible and he drew it forth with a strange tugging at his heart strings. God knows how that Bible had ever come into his chest. It was nothing that he himself cherished or would have thought of putting there. It must have been his mother who had slipped it in among the linens her hands had packed with tender care, and as he drew it forth on this particular day in the midst of that lonely island, it took his thoughts with painful vividness back home. There rose before him in a flash the rolling downs of Fifeshire, green and dotted with sheep, the great gray cliffs along the shore, and nestling beneath them in the bay, the little town of Largo. At the west end of the village there was his home, his father's cozy, homey dwelling, surrounded by its garden, and there in the lattice window sat his mother knitting, looking off to sea perhaps and longing for news of him. Unconsciously his hand caressed the Bible; he climbed the height to his look-out, sat down with the book on his lap and buried his face in his hands. He could see it all so clearly. And now there rose before him, all overgrown with ivy, so peaceful and serene, the kirk itself. He could see the light that streamed in through its stained glass windows, the congregation there in Sabbath day attire with fresh and happy faces, and over all a Sabbath air of quiet joy and calm. He could see his mother by his side, her eyes aglow with pride in him,—so much she had expected from this, her stalwart son. And then he minded how during the very services in the kirk, his hot temper had led him to start a-brawling. His mother's

eyes grew dark with shame, men thrust him out by force, and on the books of the kirk he could see the record written as with points of fire: "Alexander Selkirk, having been for his indecent behavior summoned for trial before the kirk sessions on this 27th day August, 1695, did not compear, being gone away to the seas."

Yes, that was what he had done—run away from his punishment to the seas; and, worse still, not three years agone, when he was a man grown and home once more, he had been summoned again before the kirk sessions and publicly rebuked before the whole congregation for quarreling with his brothers and raising a tumult in his father's home. Suddenly his shoulders shook with sobs and all his soul revolted against that unruly temper that had caused him so much trouble all his life. Had it not been for that same temper, he would not have been here alone and miserable on a desert island. He wept as he had not done since he was a lad at his mother's knee, and in him rose the resolution strong, henceforth to bar out that beastly fault and never let it run away with him again. The tears he shed left him greatly purified and refreshed even as the earth after a thunder storm. Slowly he opened the book on his knees and read:

"They wandered in the wilderness in a solitary way; they found no city to dwell in.

"Hungry and thirsty their soul fainted in them;

"Then they cried unto the Lord in their trouble and He delivered them out of their distresses."

And again:

"The wilderness and the solitary place shall be glad for them; and the desert shall rejoice and blossom as the rose.

"Say to them that are of a feeble heart, Be strong, fear not; behold, your God will come . . . and save you."

Suddenly those words applied to him and to his need. Misery had melted the pride of a stubborn heart, and for the first time

in his life, his thoughts drew near to the Creator of the universe. He read on and on, and with every word he read, his loneliness diminished; hope took the place of despair and more and more his spirit rose within him. At length with new vigor and purpose he closed the book and strode down from the height to his cave.

Now for him everything was changed. He realized for the first time that life on Juan Fernandez would be what he made it. If he lived miserably, doing nothing to better his condition, and pinning all his hope of happiness on the chance of a stray sail making its way toward the island at some hazy time in the future, he might waste away a lifetime in despair. Now, now was the time to conquer every adverse circumstance, live and be happy. "Behold, *now* is the accepted time," saith St. Paul. "Behold, *now* is the day of salvation."

He set to work at once. First of all he saw that he had let his cave grow filthy. He spent some time in cleaning it out and washing of clothes and bedding. As he worked he was able sometimes to whistle. Moreover it was a remarkable fact that the howling of the seals no longer annoyed him; he could even hear their voices with pleasure as furnishing a certain sense of companionship, and the change within his own spirits made him approach them in so different a manner, with such confidence and assurance that now, when occasion demanded, he could safely make his way through them. It is true loneliness and despair returned at times to tempt him, but he had henceforth always wherewithal to resist them through reading of the scriptures and thinking on the words therein set down.

Having put things in such order about his cave as they had not been in since his arrival on the island, he began next to consider the question of food. As he had been unwilling to leave the beach and living on that food the most easily procurable there, he had been eating almost nothing but turtle, till he could scarce brook the thought of turtle again. Now he arranged at stated intervals, morning and evening, to go to his look-out on the rocks, but the rest of the time he put the matter of sails out of his mind, and went about his business of providing for his natural wants. Accordingly, he traveled inland, and on the heights back from the shore found a plenty of goats. Juan Fernandez, the Spanish sailor who had first discovered the island a century or more ago and given it his name, had resided there for some time, stocking the place with goats, and the wild creatures of this time were descendants of those domestic beasts Juan Fernandez left behind at the time of his final abandonment of the island. By means of his gun, Selkirk was thus able to provide himself with goat's flesh, and he perceived that the fruit of the pimento which is the same as the Jamaica pepper and has a most delicious smell, would season his meat instead of salt. He therefore soon learned to prepare victuals he could truly relish in place of the unpalatable stuff with which his indifference had been providing him. In particular he was able to make a most excellent broth. Being still, however, greatly in want of fresh vegetables, he decided to set out and explore the island in search of the same.

He found Juan Fernandez to be about thirteen miles in length by four in width, rocky and mountainous everywhere, the mountains being covered with green to the skyline, except where precipitous faces of rock formed a beautiful contrast to the luxuriant pale vegetation. Everywhere was a great profusion of ferns, there being two varieties of tree-ferns that raised their feathery heads to the height of a good-sized tree over many an overhanging crag or precipitous ravine. The steep paths up the hills were bordered by a thicket of flowering shrubs and herbs, one of the most remarkable of the latter throwing up leaf stalks eight and ten feet in height and forming with the leaves, which frequently measured fifteen feet across, a canopy under which one could easily have ridden on horseback. In several brooks at no great distance from his cave he found water cress of an excellent flavor and to his delight, he discovered growing in great profusion among the trees of the island, the cabbage palm which yields most edible leaf buds quite after the manner of the common cabbage.

In several places he came upon the ruins of huts or shelters that had probably been erected in times past by the few sailors preceding him who had spent periods of greater or less length on the island, though never before like him alone, being always in companies of three or four. He searched well in these places, but found nothing of any value left behind, save that from one he was able to procure a few nails. In the rank growth near these ruins, however, radishes, parsnips and turnips were growing. These appeared at present to be wild, but were undoubtedly offspring of seeds originally sowed by some one of the earlier inhabitants of the island. Thus provided with a welcome addition to his food supply, Selkirk returned to his cave, a spot now quiet and serene enough since the seals had long since departed.

It was now well along in February, being the close of summer. Selkirk had long since carved on a tree the date of his arrival on the island, and by computing the number of days during which he had kept no track of the passage of time, he had from then on carried on an accurate system of markings by which he was always able to ascertain the date. With autumn coming on and winter in view, he began to think of building himself a hut. Even in that genial climate where trees were green the year around, he knew that frost was common at night in winter, snow would sometimes be found on the ground and there would be much rain, therefore he felt the need of a more habitable shelter than his cave. This he desired the more especially as he had seen from his lookout in all the time he had been on the island only one sail and that far off on the very edge of the horizon, so he felt more than ever that he was like to stay years or perhaps forever in that place.

After thinking the matter over carefully he came to this con- clusion,—he must build his hut well back from the shore in a most sheltered and inaccessible spot, for by this time his powder was gone and he had no means of defence. He was now well satisfied that no savage beasts dwelt on the island, but he had this to take into consideration,—if a boat ever did land there it was as like to hold men from whom he must flee as men into whose arms he could throw himself. He knew well enough the character of the rough adventurers who sailed those seas,—buccaneers, pirates, outlaws. Moreover at this time, France and Spain being both at war with England, to fall into the hands of Frenchman or Spaniard would have been to be captured by a foe. At length he made up his mind that if a French vessel put in he would surrender, trusting the nature of the French to deal honorably by him even though he were an enemy. But if the vessel were Spanish, he would flee and hide himself and never give up, for he knew the jealousy of Spain for England was so great that it was her acknowledged policy never to let a single Englishman return to Europe who had any knowledge of the South Seas. If he were to fall into the hands of Spanish sailors they would either kill him or make him a slave to work in their rich South American mines. This much was certain then,—he must build his hut where it would be a safe retreat in case of need. Therefore he climbed the rocks by an intricate path, and finding hidden high up among them a beautiful little glade on the edge of a spacious

wood, a spot most difficult to come at, and so concealed as to be well nigh undiscoverable, he selected that spot as the site for his hut.

By the exercise of much toil and patience, he then cut down with the small axe at his disposal, a sufficient number of pimento trees for his purpose. These he was obliged to join most accurately and carefully together by means of notches, having a great scarcity of nails. On the plains and small hills of the island there abounded a species of grass which grew to the height of seven or eight feet. This he cut most laboriously with his knife, and, on being dried, it proved to produce straw resembling that of oats. With this he thatched his hut. He then constructed a framework for a bed, covered it with straw and spread thereon his bed clothes, to sleep on which was a most welcome change after months of lying on the hard ground. Being still uncertain whether or no his hut was weather-proof, he hung the walls on the inside with well tanned skins of goats.

He had now for some time, since he had used the last of his powder, been presented with a new problem in the matter of procuring his goats. Being determined however to be overcome of no adverse circumstance, he one day made after a goat on foot. The creature was too fleet for him, but a young kid crossing his path, he found himself able to overtake that and seize it with his bare hands, and as he daily exercised to increase his speed, he was soon able to overtake the grown goats as well. He made after them first as they slackened speed to climb an ascent, but with gradual practice and owing to the moderate and temperate life he led, which kept him in fine bodily trim, he was at last able to run down even the fleetest goats at full speed on the level.

With the poor tools at his command, it took him many weeks to build his hut which he made of a spacious size. But this hut being complete, he found his energy by no means flagging, and

# THE TREASURE CHEST

ere the rainy season began he built at no great distance from it a second and smaller hut wherein he might cook his victuals.

Thus when winter came he was well prepared to meet it. The weather was never tempestuous, but there was some frost and snow, a little hail and great quantities of rain. In the larger hut he slept and passed the long periods of downpour. It had openings for windows which rendered it exceedingly light and pleasant, and over these openings in case of need to keep out the rain or cold could be dropped the goat skin coverings. Here within, he was cozy and snug enough, and he led a most orderly and comfortable life, instituting there the simple but beautiful form of family worship to which he had been accustomed in his father's home. Soon after he left his bed and before be began the duties of the day, he sang a psalm, then read a portion of the scriptures, finishing with devout prayer. Moreover he always repeated his devotions aloud in order to hear the sound of a human voice and retain his ability to speak the English tongue. The remainder of his time he occupied himself with making various articles of furniture and carving dishes and utensils out of wood, also in studying his books on navigation.

The winter offered but one incident of any importance and that was the coming up onto the beach early in July of great quantities of sea-lions. These strange creatures differ little in shape of body from seals but they are larger (being sometimes twenty feet long and of two tons weight). They have another sort of skin, their fur being shorter and coarser than that of the seal, and their heads are much larger in proportion, with very large mouths, monstrous big eyes and exceedingly heavy whiskers, the hair of which is stiff enough to make tooth pickers. These creatures stayed from July to September and were never observed during that time to go into the water but lay covering the shore above a musket shot from the water-side. But by this time Selkirk was in such good spirits that he was quite able to make his way safely through them whenever he needed to approach the shore.

With the return of spring, he found himself in a very different state of mind from what he had been the year before. When the rains ceased and it began to bud and twitter without, his heart leaped up and was glad within him. In the woods nearby the flowers appeared and there was a sort of blackbird with a red vest that came most tamely about his dwelling. Moreover, as the season advanced, there was scarcely a plant of myrtle or of a shrub with long dark bells like the myrtle, which was not inhabited by a pair of vari-colored humming birds, no bigger than bumble bees, and these little creatures whirring and buzzing over the flowers filled Selkirk with delight.

The fall before he had carefully collected seeds of the vegetables that grew in different parts of the island, and this spring he cultivated a goodly patch of ground near his hut, having no implement with which to till the ground save his knife and axe. Here he planted a garden which he kept free of weeds and in most excellent and orderly condition.

His one trouble now was that he was greatly pestered with rats, his hut being overrun with the vermin and they so bold as to gnaw his clothes and even his feet when sleeping. On considering how to rid himself of this pest, he determined to catch and tame some of the wild cats that inhabited the island. These creatures, though of a uniform yellowish gray color like the real wildcat were not in truth that creature, as might be told from their smaller size and from their tails which were thin and tapered at the end, while the wildcat's tail is bushy and of uniform size throughout. They, like the rats, were descendants of domestic creatures that had got ashore from some boat or other that had put in in times past to wood and water at the island. Nevertheless, though they were offspring of the tamest of beasts, they were as fierce and wild as wildcats and of an agility that made them well nigh impossible to catch, so quickly could they slip out of one's very grasp and up into the trees. They formed their nests in rocky crevices or hollow trees and when disturbed there, would rise up and give fight, snarling and spitting fiercely, every hair on their bodies bristling with rage. Selkirk, however, was able to procure some kitlings which through patient care and feeding he tamed, and these being grown, speedily delivered him from the rats and kept his hut clean of the pests ever after.

Having succeeded well in taming the cats, he began also to tame kids that he might have food within easy reach in case of need. In this wise his hut was soon surrounded with tame creatures.

Pursuing goats up the mountainsides was by no means without danger, for the soil at any great height was very light and shallow, the vegetation being mostly a scrubby undergrowth, and if a man seized hold of this to help himself up the slope, the whole was like to give way, come up by the roots and precipitate him down the steep. Once Selkirk so eagerly pursued a goat that he catched hold of it on the brink of a precipice of which he was not aware, the bushes having hid it from him. So he fell over from a great height with the goat under him and lay at the bottom of the cliffs for a matter of twenty-four hours before he came to his senses—the amount of which time he calculated by the change in the moon since last he observed it. Having then crawled a mile back to

his cottage, he there remained some ten days ere he was able to stir out again.

As time passed he began to be greatly troubled that, with so much using, his knife was worn clean to the heft. He mourned beyond measure the loss of so valuable and necessary an implement. One day, however, as he wandered on the beach, keeping a sharp lookout as he always did for aught that might be of use, what should he spy, half buried in the sand, but some iron hoops. Doubtless they had been cast away by some ship as altogether unworthy, but to him they were a treasure then more priceless than a shipload of Spanish gold. Taking them back to his hut, he there broke off a piece, beat it thin, and ground the edge upon stones. Thus by the exercise of a little ingenuity, he was able to provide himself with a knife.

The knife, as may well be believed, was not the only one of his belongings that wore out. In course of time his clothes did likewise. He then made himself a coat, cap and breeches of goatskin with the hair outside. These he stitched together with little thongs of leather which he cut from the skins and attached to a nail. Having a plenty of linen cloth by him, thanks to the care of his mother, he sewed himself shirts when his wore out, using the nail again for a needle, and for thread the worsted that he unravelled from an old pair of stockings. As his bedding gave way, he replaced that also by goatskins. Only with the wearing through of his shoes did he find here an article that he could not replace. Nevertheless, as he was forced to shift without them, he found his feet grow so hard, he could run anywhere, even over the sharp jagged rocks, without the slightest annoyance. Thus even the loss of his shoes remained no great inconvenience.

One day as he stood on his look-out scanning the sea for a sail (it must have been about in the second year of his solitude) he did indeed, to the joy of his soul, see a sail bearing straight for the island. Leaving all else, he stayed at the lookout, never taking his eyes off the ship, his heart beating high with hope. But as it drew well within the range of vision, he saw to his dismay that it was a high and clumsy vessel, its stem and stern built up like castles,—Spanish without a doubt. Now as he had fully made up his mind rather to stay forever on the island than fall into the hands of the Spaniards, he watched until he made sure they were going to land, and then retired at once to his inaccessible retreat, where he stayed quietly, never once moving out of it so long as they remained on the island. From among the rocks he kept a sharp lookout over their encampment below, and he found the sight of human kind and the sound of their voices so agreeable even though he knew them to be enemies of a fierce and relentless kind, that he was often almost compelled to go down and join them. More than once some of the men strayed up the rocks straight in the direction of his hut, but fortunately he had built it so far beyond the distance of any easy climb that they never penetrated so far. At last, having taken aboard wood and water, they made off and Selkirk found himself once more the solitary master of the isle.

Curiously enough, it was not many months later, that he again espied a ship coming toward the island. This time, however, she was not of so distinct a type that he could at once decide whether she was Spanish or French. Desiring a closer examination, he ran eagerly down toward the beach, and was proceeding along through the underbrush with insufficient caution, when he suddenly came straight upon several of the crew before he even so much as knew they had landed. On the instant he perceived they were Spanish and made off. The others were struck dumb with astonishment at coming suddenly on so wild appearing a man on what they had believed to be an uninhabited island. However, they recovered themselves at once, fired shots after him and followed hot on his heels. They being close upon him, he suddenly shinned up a tree and hid himself in its branches. The Spaniards pursued him to the very foot of the tree and there losing track of him lingered long on the spot just beneath him. They even looked up frequently into the branches and Selkirk's heart went pounding, for had they perceived him, he could scarcely have got out of range of their firelocks, but so dense were the leaves they did not discover him and at length they retired once more to their camp.

Henceforth, after his disappointment in this second ship, Selkirk seemed even less than ever to set his heart on leaving the island. And indeed after this no other ship again came near.

He dwelt now in a state of great cheerfulness and even joy, not only reconciled to his lot but taking much pleasure in it. For the greater part of the year the sky was cheerful and serene, the air temperate and his little hut was on the edge of a spacious wood abloom with flowers. He kept it always clean and well-ordered and had even come to ornament it with the fragrant green boughs of trees, so that it formed a delicious bower around which played soft and balmy breezes. It grew to seem to him much like home and he came back to it always after an absence with that pleasant warming of the inner man always experienced by one coming home. Moreover his cats and tame kids became exceedingly dear to his heart. Though he had at first thought of taming them only to meet his own physical needs, he soon found himself grown mightily fond of the little creatures, and as they grew to love him in return, they in some measure satisfied that natural craving for companionship and affection which dwells ever deep in the heart of man. The kids would come leaping to meet him, licking his hands almost like dogs and the cats would rub against his legs and vie with one another to curl up purring in his lap. He would amuse himself often by teaching his pets

to dance and do tricks, singing rousing old songs, and himself
dancing with them to the music of his own voice. It was a strange
and pretty sight, that!—the great man in his rough and shaggy
garments, his face softened with joy of the little creatures, dancing
and springing about in their midst, as though they were friends
all speaking one language, the language of love that is foreign to
none of God's creatures.

Selkirk had his garden, too, and indeed by application of his
wits conquered all the inconveniences of his solitude. For food
he had all he could wish for of variety and profusion right at
hand,—goat's flesh and milk, turtle, crawfish, fish, turnips,
parsnips, radishes, cabbage, watercress, and a variety of small
but delicious black plum, the only article of his diet now not
easily procurable, for they grew in places hard to come at high
up in the mountains, but were sufficiently delicious to repay the
effort of gathering them. He perceived, too, that taste is much
a matter of habit, for he had grown to relish his food seasoned with

pimento quite as well as when he had it seasoned with salt.

The wood of the pimento he used entirely for firewood and as it burned, it gave off a most delicious fragrance and served him both for warmth and candle, throwing up a splendid blaze that lit all the darkness about. He was by this time intimately familiar with all the little by-paths of his mountain kingdom and could bound from crag to crag and slip down precipices with the utmost confidence.

So as he surveyed all the beauty and comfort about him and recalled the misery of his earlier state on the island, it seemed to him that his own change of heart had indeed made the promise come true,—"The wilderness and the solitary place shall be glad for them and the desert shall rejoice and blossom as the rose."

He no longer missed the society of men. The strife and struggle of humankind seemed far away; God seemed very near. He read: "Behold the hour cometh, yea is now come that ye . . . shall leave me alone, and yet I am not alone because the Father is with me." And as he stood beneath the calm and smiling sky, with the beauty of all out-doors about, and the sea stretching endlessly before him, he felt such a sense of nearness to the great Spirit of the universe, as he had never known in all his life before, and his thoughts were full of reverence and simple childlike peace.

For four years and four months he stayed there, and then one day, the thirty-first of January, 1709, it was, he was as usual surveying the water when he descried two vessels approaching. As they drew near, he saw for a certainty they were English. It was then late in the afternoon and he kept his eyes fixed on them until dark, though he scarcely felt any elation of spirit, as he might had they come some time earlier. After nightfall he gathered plenty of pimento wood and made a great fire to signal the vessels that there was some one alive on the island. All night long he tended it, but he spent none of the time in anxious suspense. Indeed, he thought far more of dressing goat's flesh wherewith to entertain the crew on the morrow, wearied as he knew they must be through months of confinement to salt provisions, than of whether or no his exile was at last to be ended.

During the night he fancied he heard from the vessels the sound of cannon, and later it appeared that his fire had occasioned the greatest surprise and alarm on shipboard. It being believed that the island was uninhabited, the English at once concluded there must be French ships at anchor in the harbor. They had earlier sent out their pinnace to reconnoiter the island, and on seeing the blaze, at once fired the quarter deck gun and several muskets to signal her to return. Then they stood all night to their quarters with decks cleared for action in case the French made at them. As they were forced to get wood and water at any price, they did not sail away, but in the morning made into the bay where they expected to see the boats of the enemy. Finding the coast clear, however, and no sign of ships anywhere, one of the vessels let down her yawl about noon and sent it ashore. Selkirk saw the boat leave the vessel and he at once tied a piece of old linen to a pole and waved it to attract their attention. As the yawl drew near, he saw it contained eight men and heard them call to him asking where was a good place to land. He pointed out the same, and, hurrying there ahead of them, stood ready to receive them as they sprang ashore. At the moment of actually meeting with humankind again, he felt a momentary joy and embraced them each in turn. He then learned that the two vessels were the Duke and Duchess under command of Captain Woodes Rogers, and he invited the sailors hospitably to his hut, but its access was so difficult and intricate, that Captain Dover and his men soon gave over trying to make it, one, Mr. Fry, alone accompanying him there. On the beach Selkirk

entertained the sailors in the best manner he could with the goat's flesh he had prepared. As the men were long absent from their boat, the Duke sent out her pinnace to see what had become of her yawl, suspecting that if there were no French ships in the bay, there might at least be a Spanish garrison lurking somewhere about. The sailors from the pinnace discovered nothing worse than the eight men from the yawl feasting on shore with a wild man, and, perceiving on closer examination that the wild man had an expression kindly, serious, and yet cheerful, they concluded him to be none such dangerous creature as they had at first supposed and invited him to return with them on board. Accordingly, he did so, bearing roast goat's flesh for the crew. As he dined with the Captain it was a remarkable fact that he no longer relished food seasoned with salt, but found himself obliged to acquire again what he had believed to be a perfectly natural taste.

After he had recounted his adventures the renowned Captain Dampier who knew him of old and was then on board as pilot, gave him so good a character that he was at once invited to sail with the Duke as mate. In the afternoon the ships cleared and the sails were taken ashore to be mended, while all hands set to work to lay in wood and provisions. Men were sent with a bull dog to capture goats, but to the surprise of everyone, Selkirk outdistanced them all, even the dog, caught the goats with his hands and bore two of them back on his shoulders.

The Duke and Duchess remained at the island till February the twelfth refitting the ships and getting in stores, and then at last the day came when Selkirk must bid farewell to his little home in the glade, to all his beloved pets, and each spot that had grown dear to him. Whether he truly rejoiced or no, when it came to the actual point of leave-taking, who knows? Who knows?

At length there he was again on shipboard and the coast of Juan Fernandez lay behind him, fading fast into mist and dreams.

He was two years still from home and on the Duke showed no more of that quarrelsome disposition that had before wrought him so much trouble. The Duke took many prizes and was most successful in its ventures against the Spanish tyrants. In several instances Selkirk was entrusted with the command of small parties sent ashore, where the property and person of the inhabitants were at his mercy, and in all such cases he showed by his mild and considerate behavior, especially towards women, that the exalted thoughts of his solitude were not of the kind to vanish.

The Duke and Duchess reached London, October 14, 1711, and Selkirk found himself, when the prize was divided, a rich man. He returned at once to Largo and a joyful reunion with his mother, father and brothers. But ever after he had no love for great companies of men, choosing rather solitude and the company of his own thoughts. Moreover he often longed for his pets and his peaceful island where he had felt so near to his Creator, nor did the luxuries riches could provide make him one whit happier than when his wants were confined to the simplest necessities and these supplied by his own efforts alone.

"I am now worth eight hundred pounds," he would often say, "but shall never be so happy as when I was not worth a farthing."


### SOLITUDE

There is a pleasure in the pathless woods,
    There is a rapture on the lonely shore,
There is society where none intrudes
    By the deep sea, and music in its roar.
                            —*Lord Byron.*

## Young Midshipman David Farragut

WHEN the War of 1812 broke out, wherein the United States found herself compelled to establish by force of arms her freedom on the seas which had been over and over again violated by England, the frigate Essex, 146 feet long, 32 short-range guns, was placed under the command of Captain David Porter. He came aboard bringing with him as midshipman his little adopted son, David Farragut, who was one day to be known as America's greatest admiral. David had received his first appointment as midshipman in the United States navy at the mature age of nine, and he was now at the time of entering on his duties aboard the Essex exactly ten.

Scarcely had the Essex put to sea when adventures began. Captain Porter captured from the midst of a whole convoy of British transports a merchantman with two hundred men, and soon after a British man-of-war, the sloop Alert of twenty guns. The two ships were taken in tow, but their officers and a number of the men were ordered as prisoners aboard the Essex. Thus the Essex soon became dangerously overcrowded, her prisoners far outnumbering the members of her crew.

Among the prisoners a conspiracy was hatched to fall unexpectedly on the Americans, either kill or overpower them and so capture the frigate. On the night when the mutiny was to break out, little midshipman Farragut lay awake in his hammock. Suddenly he saw a man looming up above him and covering him with his pistol. For a moment the man gazed intently at him to make certain he was asleep, ready to shoot without mercy at a sign of the smallest movement. The boy never budged, but through half open lids he saw that the sailor was one of the British prisoners, and with remarkable keenness of wit, he guessed what was afoot on the vessel. When the Englishman, satisfied that he was asleep, stole away, David slipped noiselessly out of his hammock and made straight off to Captain Porter, dodging well out of sight of the gathering mutineers.

The Captain was asleep in his cabin when the boy broke into the room, but at first news of the mutiny, he was instantly on his feet. Perceiving in a flash the only way to save the ship, Porter rushed, half dressed as he was, onto the deck, shouting, "Fire! Fire! Fire!" The effect was wonderful. The mutineers were at once confused and alarmed, fear of fire at sea driving all thoughts of mutiny out of their heads, while the American crew remarkably well disciplined in fire drill, came tumbling up on deck and rushed each to his station with a cutlass in one hand and a blanket in the other. This sudden and unexpected appearance of the crew in perfect fighting array, finished the demoralization of the mutineers. At Captain Porter's orders, they were every one seized and secured. Thus by his coolness and keenness of wit, little midshipman Farragut's first adventure at sea was to save a ship to the American navy. The next required a still greater display of manliness and courage.

Late in the winter of 1812 the Essex was ordered on a cruise through the South Atlantic around Cape Horn and into the Pacific, there to attack the extensive fishing interests of Great Britain, to rescue any American boats and to set free captured American whalers. The proper season for rounding Cape Horn had long since passed and the course of the Essex would lie through a region exceedingly tempestuous in winter. Moreover the ports along the coast were all friendly to England, and the Essex could not hope to refit or revictual in any of their harbors. She would have to depend solely on her own resources. Undaunted by the perils that lay before them, Captain Porter and his crew, little David Farragut among them, set out upon this distant cruise in the last days of January, 1813.

As the Essex neared the Horn, the most violent storms broke over her, lifting the waves into raging mountains of water and hurling them against the frail little boat with gigantic force. But in spite of all dangers and hardships she kept resolutely on. At length she sighted the rocky, barren shore of the Ga-la'pa-gos Islands off the coast of Ecuador, which Porter had learned were the favorite rendezvous for the British whalers. Here they cruised about in a leisurely fashion, little David and other members of the crew frequently going ashore to fish, hunt the huge tortoises for which the place was famous, or to pick the luscious Galapagos pears. But as the British whalers appeared in these waters, they captured them all successively till at last every single one had fallen a victim to the Essex and numerous American prisoners had been freed from the hands of the enemy. Captain Porter then found himself with nine vessels under him and such a number of prisoners that he was obliged to put back to the mainland of Ecuador and make preparations to send the prize ships he had taken back for safe keeping to the harbor of Valparaiso, Chile, one of the few South American ports that was friendly to the United States. One of these prizes which had been turned into a United States cruiser and christened The Essex Junior, he detailed as escort to the convoy on the return. He then ordered each of his officers as prizemaster to command one of the captured vessels, but not having officers enough to go around, he found himself forced to select some one among the crew to command the American ship Barclay which he had recaptured from the enemy. His choice for this responsible task fell on Midshipman Farragut. With a party of seamen under him, the boy was sent aboard, having orders to manage the Barclay on her long voyage to Chile. Imagine it! At the age of twelve in command of a vessel. It was a tremendously important event, and the boy was rightfully proud of the confidence reposed in him.

The Captain of the Barclay, who had been in command when the vessel was captured by the enemy, was a huge Yankee from New Bedford, a violent tempered old fellow, and he was furious at being superseded by a "nutshell of a boy" as he contemptuously called young David. For such an old sea-dog to be placed under the orders of a twelve-year-old boy seemed galling enough to his pride and he secretly determined to put the young whippersnapper in his proper place the very moment the other ships had departed. Accordingly, when the Essex Junior and the convoy made off to southward, and Captain Porter had disappeared to the northward, the Captain of the Barclay still kept his vessel contemptuously at anchor, making no preparations to follow, and flaunting his intention of remaining where he was exactly so long as it pleased him.

Little Midshipman Farragut saw that his hour of trial had come. He must play the man now and assume the command entrusted to him, order the ship under way and see her off on her journey, or else acknowledge himself too little to fulfill the responsibility Captain Porter had laid upon him, yield up his

command and let the Captain have his own way ever after. Though he secretly shook in his boots like every one else in the presence of the grizzly old fellow, he nevertheless went straight to him and ordered quietly: "Have the maintopsail filled away, and close up at once with the convoy."

At this the Captain burst forth in a fury. He would go where he pleased and when he pleased. He would steer for New Zealand or the moon if he liked! And he cried out to the sailors standing about:

"Let no man dare touch a rope without my orders. I'll shoot if you do. I've no mind to trust myself with a damned little nutshell! I'll go my own course and shoot the dog who takes orders from any but me."

Unfortunately, however, he did not have his pistols with him to carry out this magnificent threat, so he plunged down the companionway after them. The men stood about irresolute. It was a moment for great decision. Little Farragut turned to his right hand man of the crew.

"Have the maintopsail filled away!" he repeated with still more positive emphasis. His pluck turned the tide with the men.

# THE TREASURE CHEST

"Ay, ay, sir," came the sailor's cheerful response, and from that time on, young David was undisputed master of the vessel. He at once set vigorously about giving all necessary orders to make sail, and calmly notified the Captain below not to come on deck with his pistols unless he wished to go overboard! The Captain, perceiving that the crew remained faithful to the little officer detailed them, and that David would in truth have no difficulty whatever in having him pitched over into the sea, decided in the interests of his own continued health and well-being to draw in his horns and obey. Thus on the long voyage back to Chile, David was in command and he carried out that great responsibility with a skill, good judgment and self-reliance, and yet with a freedom from all conceit or unnecessary self-assertion which was remarkable in a lad of twelve.

The little "nutshell" was assuredly given plenty of opportunity to prove his mettle aboard the Essex, for when after faithfully performing his mission he once more returned on the Essex Junior to join that vessel at the Galapagos Islands, it was with news that the British government had been so aroused by tales of the destruction the Essex had wrought to her commerce and fisheries in the Pacific, that she was sending out the frigate Phoebe and two sloops to capture her.

On hearing this, Captain Porter at once sailed westward to the Mar-que'sas Islands where he could overhaul the Essex without danger from British men-of-war and make ready for the coming struggle with a greatly superior force.  Here the Essex and Essex Junior lay for six months. The crews were daily drilled in the use of the guns, cutlasses and muskets and trained with that perfect discipline for which Captain Porter was famous.

During this time, David and the other midshipmen, when not at their studies or drill, were allowed ashore, where they gathered bananas, yams, bread-fruit and cocoanuts, and made friends with the sturdy brown native boys, who taught them to throw the spear, walk on stilts and especially to perform many wonderful feats in swimming.

At last, all preparations being made, the Essex and Essex Junior returned to Valparaiso Harbor, arriving on the twenty-third of February, 1814. Five days later the frigate Phoebe and the sloop Cherub appeared in the bay. Half the crew of the Essex were ashore at the time on leave, and Captain Hillyar of the Phoebe, being informed of this, at once determined to seize her while she must fall an easy prey, in spite of the fact that Valparaiso Harbor was neutral water where no hostile engagements could lawfully occur. But Captain Porter had been on the look-out. A signal gun brought every one of his men in fifteen minutes back to his station. When the Phoebe came dashing up within fifteen feet of the Essex, Captain Hillyar, instead of finding a vessel at his mercy, to his intense surprise, found every American at his gun, with matches burning and cutlasses drawn, in such a formidable state of defence that he speedily backed away, and tried to pass off his hostile approach with some clumsy compliments to Captain Porter. Captain Porter replied to his compliments with a politeness so grim that the Phoebe was more than ever anxious to get out of his reach and in her haste to accomplish this, she placed herself in such a position that Captain Porter could easily have raked her fore and aft with his guns and done for her once for all. But his principles of honor forbade him to violate the neutrality of the harbor, so he let the Phoebe go free, though he later discovered to his immense cost that Captain Hillyar was not a man to return such an act of courtesy.

The English ships, after provisioning, went outside the harbor and maintained a blockade of the two American vessels.

# THE TREASURE CHEST

Week after week they cruised up and down just outside the bay, so that the Americans could not possibly slip through.

On March twenty-eighth, a heavy gale swept into the harbor and Porter decided to take advantage of the weather to run the blockade. At first it looked as though he would succeed, but on her way the Essex was struck by a violent squall that carried away her maintopsail. Escape in such a disabled state was impossible, so Porter tried to regain his safe position in the harbor, but the Essex was only able to struggle as far back as a small bay about a quarter of a mile off shore. She was, however, still within neutral waters and had every reason to expect that Hillyar would respect that neutrality, remembering how Porter had refused to fire on him when he had the Phoebe so entirely at his mercy. But Porter soon saw his mistake. As soon as the British discerned the plight of the Essex, the two vessels both bore down together on the crippled frigate, now separated from her companion, and opened their broadsides on her. Then began one of the most nobly contested defences in history, the odds being from the beginning three to one against the Essex.

Through the frightful scenes that followed, Midshipman Farragut bore himself like a man, now carrying messages for Captain Porter, now helping with a gun, now fetching powder, now supporting a wounded man down below. Once he was knocked down a hatch by the explosion of a cannon ball. Again a shot tore away one of his coat-tails, but still the little midshipman remained at his post in the midst of the fray. At length fire broke out on the ship, and was nearing the powder magazine. Men came running up from below with their clothing on fire. Captain Porter ordered them to jump overboard and swim for their lives. Then, finding that the ship was in a sinking condition, he surrendered in order to save the wounded.

On the following day, David Farragut went aboard the Phoebe, a prisoner, and was sent into the steerage with the British middies. He was almost in tears over the capture of the Essex, but was roused from his grief by the sight of an English midshipman calmly appropriating his—David's—beloved pet pig Murphy.

"That's my pig!" shrieked David, seizing Murphy by the ear.

"Fight for it then!" jeered the others.

Without more ado David stripped off his jacket and pitched into the young Englishman in short order, with such excellent results that in a few moments he had most soundly and satisfactorily trounced him. Thereafter he took Master Murphy under his arm and walked off, feeling that he had thus in some degree wiped out the disgrace of the American defeat!

Soon after this, David was sent back to America with the other officers on parole, and thus ended his connection with the famous frigate Essex, whereon he got the training that years later in the war for the preservation of the American Union, made possible the splendid victories of New Orleans and Mobile Bay,— victories won against almost impossible odds by the man that grew out of that self-same boy who was midshipman David Farragut.

## Princess Nelly and The Seneca Chief*
### A True Story

IN the days of the American Revolution, the whole of western Pennsylvania was inhabited by different tribes of Indians. Of these, the Delawares were friends of the whites and took part with the United States; the Iroquois, on the contrary, were friends and allies of England. Very few white settlers had ventured into those parts at that time, for the life of frontiersmen amid such roving bands of hostile red men was one of constant peril and alarm. Even those who felt themselves in some measure protected by their friendly neighbors, the Delawares, never lost sight of the caution required by their exposed position.

Only in the vicinity of the military garrison at Pittsburgh, or Fort Pitt as it was then called, was there any sense of security among the settlers. Here on the banks of the Plum River, a tributary of the Alleghany, there settled one Mr. Lytle, from Baltimore, with his wife and children. For some time they lived in uneventful comfort, experiencing no hostile visits from the Indians. The neighbors, it is true, having had more experience of frontier life, and being therefore more awake to the cunning and unexpected nature of the savages, had more than once annoyed Mr. Lytle by false alarms, till he had come to believe the stories of danger entirely exaggerated, visions called up by weak and foolish fear; and he quite relaxed his own vigilance, sinking into an easy going sense of security.

One day in the autumn of 1779, he set out early in the morning with all his serving men to help a neighbor at some distance raise a new building on his farm, thereby leaving his wife and children without a single man to protect them. After the noonday meal, Maggie and Tom, the two younger children, aged four and six respectively, went out to romp in the garden. Eleanor,

*This is a story of the little girl who later became Mrs. John Kinzie, one of the earliest settlers of Chicago.

or Nelly, the oldest, a pretty child of nine, and her brother, two years younger, were at play in a little wooded hollow in the rear of their father's house. Around them lay great trees of the forest, which Mr. Lytle had recently felled, with branches still untrimmed, and over these they climbed with merry laughter.

It was an afternoon of glowing splendor; the meadows swam in golden haze, the hillsides loomed aloft in gold with fleeting purple shadows, the river swept its shining path through banks of flaming autumn color, and over all there seemed to lie a wondrous golden peace. Behind the children, in the cabin, could be heard the voice of their mother as she sang at her work. No scene could have appeared more homelike and serene. But suddenly Nelly stopped short in the midst of her play and clutched her brother wildly by the shoulder.

"Look," she whispered, "behind that log."

The boy peered off in the direction which his sister had indicated. Behind the green and untrimmed boughs of one of those fallen forest giants, what was it moving?—a squirrel, a fawn, or was it a red face?—a gaily colored bird or a clump of colored feathers on the head of a savage Indian?

The boy answered not a word. Seizing his sister by the hand, he dragged her off toward the house. The children were accustomed to seeing friendly Delawares about the place. These good Indians now and again made them visits, and some among them the Lytle family held in the warmest affection. But then, these came honestly straight to the house; they never came lurking, sneaking, hiding. The sight Nelly and the boy had seen, indistinct though it was, had roused in their minds the memory of all those stories of Indian cruelties, with which the neighbors had delighted to regale them. Breathless, the two burst into the cabin.

"Mother," they cried and the voice of each was more shrill

than the other, "Mother, there is a strange Indian down in the hollow hiding behind the trees."

The mother looked quietly up from her knitting, half smiling, half annoyed.

"What! only one?" she said. "Usually you fancy a score at least! My dear children, when will you stop alarming us all for nothing? The neighbors' children have frightened you out of your wits with their ridiculous stories. You know quite well our farm is too near Fort Pitt for the Indians to dare give us trouble. If there be any Indian there at all, it is one of our good friends, the Delawares. When will you stop mistaking every whisk of a squirrel's tail among the leaves for a band of Indians? Go back to your play and put aside childish fears. Even your little brother and sister, out there in the garden, have not such childish fancies. You must learn to have greater courage."

Nelly and her brother hung their heads, humbled by the rebuke. It was true they had more than once before come running with false alarms, yet now they turned away with lagging feet to obey their mother. This time they felt so sure of what they had seen! The play was all gone out of them. Out past the garden they went where Maggie and Tom were at play. The two little ones giggled and hid as the older ones passed by, making strange and marvelous noises intended to frighten their elders. But Nelly and her brother paid no heed. They went slowly back to the little hollow.

A different place it seemed now from what it had been a few moments before. The golden peace had fled; a lurid loneliness brooded about, the shadows had grown fantastic. So far, so very far away it seemed from the shelter of the house. Nelly and her brother had no wish to play. They seated themselves on a fallen log and held close to each other.

"Hark!" whispered Nelly. "There's a rustling among the bushes."

Just at that moment, "Bob-white!" a quail whistled some-where near them. Almost immediately, "Bob-white!" a second note answered the first.

"It is never birds that are calling like that!" said the boy.

The children were gazing so intently before them, in the direction of the fallen log where they thought they had seen the red man, that everything else about sank out of their vision entirely. Suddenly big red hands were clapped over their mouths from behind and they felt themselves seized in an iron grasp. Then two great Indians lifted them from their feet and carried them into the forest. Behind them still faintly sounded, as if from another world, the voice of their mother singing and the ring-ing silvery laughter of little Maggie and Tom.

At some distance from the house, the Indians set the children down to walk by themselves, making grimly threatening gestures to force them to keep silence. Then they hurried them off through the forest and soon joined a band of their fellows. So tall and fierce and splendidly dressed were the captors of the children, that the little ones guessed at once they must be enemies. They could not possibly be the Delawares of the neighborhood.

For some little distance, they dragged and drove the children along in silence. The little boy whimpered once—it was a dread-ful plight to be in—but then he squared his shoulders, sniffed back his tears, flung back his head, and marched sturdily on his way. As to Nelly, now that the worst had come to pass, her spirit rose undaunted to meet it. There was no more timor-ousness about her; she took her brother's hand firmly in hers with a motherly air of protection and walked staunchly along by his side, her eyes flashing lightning if one of the Indians but showed signs of molesting the boy.

Neither child had the slightest idea what was about to happen to them, but the overcolored pictures drawn for them by their

366

neighbors made them expect the worst. Through the leafy
aisles of the forest, on and on they marched. Toward nightfall
as they drew far away from all white settlements, the Indians
somewhat relaxed the vigilant guard they had been keeping over
the children. When it began to grow dusk, they halted, made

their camp for the night, lit their camp fire, and set their watches to guard against surprise. Then the children were left to their own devices. The two sat down together on the grass at a little distance from their captors, and believing themselves no longer noticed, gave way for the first time to tears. Nelly took her little brother in her arms and the two wept together at thought of the uncertainty of their fate, of their peaceful home, and the loving mother from whom they had been torn.

Suddenly, as they gave vent to their grief, there stood before them a tall and majestic Indian of a strong and forceful countenance, yet strangely mild and gentle. Immovable though his features were, like those of all Indians, he still seemed to feel compassion for the little ones. In his strange Indian tongue with gutturals and low grunts, he even tried to soothe them. He pulled up great armfuls of the long grass that grew near their camping place and made them a bed. Then he shared with them his own stock of dried meat and parched corn and gave them to understand by signs that no further evil was intended them.

Scarcely had he settled them, somewhat calmed and comforted, on the bed he had prepared, than in the glare of the camp fire there appeared a second party of Indians belonging to the same band. As they loomed up out of the darkness, the light picked out the gaudy colors in their feathers and beads, casting the rest into deep shadow, and shone on their paint-streaked faces and chests with a gleam as of burnished copper. With them they brought a white prisoner. Her pale face, shining almost like marble in contrast to their own, stood out distinctly in the blaze against the black background of the forest. Then the children saw that the prisoner was none other than their mother.

With little shrieks of relief they ran and clung to her skirts and she covered them with kisses. The Indians did not attempt to separate them, but allowed the mother to go off with the children to the couch that had been prepared for them. Then the mother told the little ones how the Indians had fallen upon her while she was at work, all unsuspecting of danger, and had borne her off a prisoner.

"And Maggie and Tom in the garden, where are they? What have the Indians done to them?" sobbed Nelly.

The mother bowed her head, her features working in anguish.

"I do not know," she whispered, barely commanding her trembling voice. "I do not know where my little ones are, but I hope they escaped with Lizzie." (Lizzie was the servant-maid.) "Lizzie disappeared the moment the Indians came."

Then from the depths of her heart, in her hour of terrible doubt and need, the mother called upon Him who is able to save, and felt herself strengthened and comforted.

Mrs. Lytle guessed from their peculiar manner of painting that their captors were Senecas, one of the six nations that then formed the tribe of the Iroquois. Doubtless they had left their village with the intention of falling on some band of their enemies, the Delawares, but, failing this, had satisfied themselves by capturing a few white settlers. She devoutly hoped their purpose was to hold the prisoners for ransom, and this seemed most reasonable to suppose, since no violence had been offered them.

Early the next morning the savages started once more on their march. It then appeared that the mild and compassionate Indian who had shared his supper with the children the night

before, was none other than the chief, Corn-Planter himself. Day after day they marched, but the prisoners were not ill-treated, and Corn-Planter seemed to have taken a wonderful fancy to Nelly. Again and again he took her up to ride on his horse before him, offered her some little trinket, or shared with her his food, and at nightfall he never failed to see that a couch of soft grass was prepared for her. On his marked partiality for Nelly, Mrs. Lytle built bright hopes that he would keep them all in safety and yield them up soon for ransom.

At length the party reached the picturesque little village of the Senecas, nestling mid fragrant, dusky pines, tall white oaks and spreading chestnuts, near the head waters of the Alleghany, at a place now called Olean Point in southwestern New York.

Corn-Planter at once took his prisoners to the principal lodge of the village. Herein dwelt his mother, widow of the former chief, a dignified, stately old woman, who was called by the rest the Old Queen. To her Corn-Planter said:

"Take the white woman and her children and treat them kindly. Many horses and guns will be given to buy them back."

But when Mrs. Lytle and her children had left the lodge, he added: "My mother, I bring to you the little white girl to take the place of the brother who was killed by the Lenape six moons ago. She shall be to you a daughter, to me a sister, and she shall dwell in our lodge forever. The boy and his mother may be bought for a ransom, but little sister shall be ours. Her they shall never have again."

So the Old Queen took Nelly to her heart in place of the little boy she had lost, and showed her every sign of affection that an Indian can display. Moreover, as her son had commanded, she provided for the prisoners every comfort made possible by the simple manner of life in the village. Thus hope rose still higher in the bosom of Mrs. Lytle and her children. Alas! they knew not that the very fondness on which they founded their brightest hopes for freedom meant the most serious barrier to any chance of liberation for Nelly.

Meantime, late in the evening of the day when Mrs. Lytle and the children had been captured, the father came whistling home. No lights in the windows of the house! Within, no fire on the hearth, no kettle simmering above with grateful aroma of the evening meal, not a single human being anywhere about! Only the mother's knitting hastily dropped in a chair, and a dilapidated rag doll deserted in a corner!

Alarmed beyond measure, the unhappy father hastened off to his nearest neighbor, who lived at a considerable distance. His calls, as he pounded on their door and frantically begged for news, aroused them from their sleep. They had no tidings to give him, but one and all, they joined in the search for the missing ones.

At length, in the house of another neighbor, they found the servant-maid. Between many tears, she managed to tell Mr. Lytle how the Indians had descended upon the house. At the first alarm, she said, she had run to an outer kitchen and hidden under a large brewing tub. There she had remained until the departure of the Indians, when she fled at once to a place of safety. All she knew concerning the family was that her mistress had been carried off and doubtless the children too, but that, so far as she had observed, no violence had been offered them.

The father and his neighbors then continued the whole night long to scour the neighborhood, searching everywhere about. Towards morning Mr. Lytle remembered an old settler who lived all alone far up the valley. To his cabin he and his friends immediately went, and from him they learned that, as he was at work in his field just before sunset, he had observed a party of strange Indians passing at some distance from him. As they wound along the brow of the hill, their forms clearly silhouetted against the sky, he could see that they had with them a prisoner who was a white woman. Here, the miserable father felt sure was news of his wife at last, and he determined to go at once with his friends to Fort Pitt, to ask advice and assistance of the Commandant and Indian agent there.

Accordingly they proceeded down the valley just as the sun was rising. On their way they came suddenly upon a hut which they had searched the night before and found apparently deserted. To their surprise they now saw standing on the high bank before it a little boy and girl holding fast to each others' hands. Mr. Lytle at once recognized his two youngest children, Maggie and Tom, and in another moment they were fast in his arms and pouring out their tale in his ears.

"We were in the garden, father," cried the boy, "when the Indians came, so many Indians, into the yard right by the house!"

"An' 'en," sobbed the little girl, "Tommy he pulled me over the fence, an' we hided ourselves in the bushes and runned an' runned so far! An' where's my mother? I want my mother!"

It appeared that the boy, who was only six years of age, had indeed shown the most remarkable courage, devotion and intelligence in saving himself and his sister from the red men. He had on the very first alarm half pulled and half pushed the little girl over the fence into a neighboring field overrun with blackberry bushes and wild raspberry. Here they hid themselves, having the sense and self-command to make no outcry at all until all was quiet and no Indians in sight, when they attempted to force a way through the field in a direction opposite to the house. Unfortunately, the little girl in her play in the garden had pulled off her shoes and stockings, and the ground being very rough, uneven, and covered with briers, she soon found her feet so cut and bruised, that she sank to the ground and declared she could not go a single step further. Then the boy took off his own

stockings, put them on her feet, and gave her also his shoes, himself going barefoot over the torturing ground.

The little creature obediently tried to scuffle along in the shoes so many sizes too large, but they kept slipping off altogether so she could not possibly wear them. Then the boy took back the shoes, but he stuck faithfully by his sister, patiently coaxing and encouraging her on, lifting her over the roughest spots and part of the time half carrying her.

Thus they made their way at length out of the field and into an unenclosed pasture ground. Here, to their great delight, they saw some cows, securely and peacefully feeding. These cows, as they knew, belonged to an old woman named Granny Myers who lived some little distance away. But in what direction from the pasture her cottage lay, they had not the slightest idea. With a wisdom that might have done credit to a grown man, the boy said: "Let's hide ourselves until sunset. Then the cows will go home and we can follow them."

Accordingly, this was what the children did, but when they reached Granny Myers' hut, in the wake of the lowing cattle, what was their dismay to find the house close-locked and deserted. The old woman had been called by some business down the valley and did not return that night. Tired and hungry, Maggie and Tom could go no further. With much effort they managed to get a few drops of milk from the cows, then laid themselves down to sleep under an old bedstead that stood behind the house. When their father and his searching party approached the place during the night, they had occasioned fresh terror to the children, who mistook the shouts and calls by means of which the searchers sought to arouse the inmates of the house, for the whoop of Indians, and, far from revealing themselves, they had crept closer together and kept as far out of sight as possible. When found in the morning they were debating what step to take next in order to reach safety.

Mr. Lytle, having then placed his two youngest children in security at Fort Pitt, told his tale to the Commandant there, who was readily interested in the matter and furnished the father with a detachment of soldiers to aid in the search. Circumstances soon pointed to the Senecas as the probable marauders, and the relief party at once directed their search among the villages of that tribe. It was necessary, however, to make their inquiries with the greatest caution, for all the tribes of the Iroquois being allies of Great Britain, were decidedly hostile to the Americans. Thus a long time passed before the father reached the village of Corn-Planter on the head waters of the Alleghany.

What was his unspeakable joy to find here his wife and the two older children. At once he began to enter into negotiations with Corn-Planter for ransoming his family. Mrs. Lytle and the boy?—Yes, Corn-Planter readily agreed on a price for them and set them free at once, but Nelly!—No, never! She was the adopted child of the tribe, she was his sister! He had taken her to supply to his mother the place of the little brother who was gone; she was dear to him and he would not part with her. To every entreaty of the father and mother, even of Nelly herself, to every increase of the price offered for the child, Corn-Planter only grunted, "Ugh! Ugh!" and shook his head with decision.

At length, finding every effort useless, the father was compelled to take his sorrowful departure, and set out once more for home with such of his loved ones as he had been fortunate enough to recover. Little Nelly threw herself into the arms of her father and mother almost in despair as they bade each other a last farewell, and the hearts of all were heavy with grief. But there was nothing else to be done, and the mother could only commend the child with a simple faith which was all that could possibly give her comfort in such an hour of trial, to the tender mercy and care of the Father of all. Then Mr. and Mrs. Lytle and their son set out on their melancholy journey homeward, trusting that some future attempt would be more effectual in recovering their daughter.

Never for a moment did Mr. Lytle relax his efforts in Nelly's behalf. He left his family in Pittsburgh, and then, hoping that a British officer, as representative of a country that was the friend and ally of the Iroquois, might have more influence with Corn-Planter than those who were regarded as enemies, he undertook an expedition to the Canadian frontier, a long and dangerous enough journey in those days, hoping to gain the assistance of the British Indian Agent, Colonel Johnson. His story of what had occurred warmly interested the feelings of that benevolent officer. In spite of the fact that the United States and Great Britain were at war, Colonel Johnson saw in the grief-stricken father no enemy, but a fellow man commanding his sympathy on the grounds of their common humanity. He, therefore, promised to spare no exertions in attempting to recover little Nelly. This promise he faithfully fulfilled. As soon as the opening of the Spring made such a journey possible, he went in person to the village of Corn-Planter and made him a most splendid offer of guns and horses if he would release the child. But Corn-Planter was inexorable. He answered the British Agent as he had answered the Americans with nothing more than two grunts and a most decisive shake of his head.

So, slowly the months lengthened out into years, and still Princess Nelly dwelt in the lodge of the Old Queen, the beloved of Chief Corn-Planter, and his mother, and all the tribe. Nothing could exceed the consideration and affection with which she was treated by all. The principal seat in the lodge was reserved for her, the most delicate food was invariably saved for her, all the handsomest silver brooches and strings of wampum were used to make fine her garments; no efforts were spared to make her happy and cause her to forget her former home and dear ones.

For a long time Nelly resisted any attempts at consolation, crying out continually for her mother, but at length, as the kindness of the Indians remained unfailing, she grew somewhat more reconciled to her lot, and even happy in the great affection which Corn-Planter showered upon her. More and more, love for his little sister wound itself around the big chief's heart; more and more his tenderness for her became a part of his very being. As he followed the game in the woods, as he led his band of warriors through the pathless depths of the forest, thoughts of the little sister awaiting him by the hearth in his mother's lodge, shed a greater warmth into his life than the very warmth of the sun itself. Nelly, being by nature affectionate, the unbounded tenderness of those among whom she dwelt called forth a certain response in her heart. Though she could never cease longing for her own dear mother, she grew to regard Corn-Planter and the Old Queen with remarkable love and reverence. She learned to speak their language and even found much joy in sharing the bustling life of the village. Wherever she went about, whether gathering wild rice from the river in her little birch bark canoe, hoeing the corn in the cornfield, or playing at ball or bowl, she always displayed such ceaseless activity and unbounded energy, that the Indians gave her the name of The Ship Under Full Sail, and by that poetic title they always called her.

Thus four years passed by; four times the months rolled their slow round from the Moon of Leaves to the Moon of Snow-shoes, from the Moon of Snow-shoes to the Moon of Leaves, while Nelly dwelt in the little village on the banks of the Alleghany. Then in 1783 came the peace between the United States and Great Britain which ended the War of the Revolution. In consequence a general pacification of the Indian tribes took place and fresh hopes of recovering their daughter arose in the hearts of Mr. and Mrs. Lytle. They removed with their family to Fort Niagara, near which was the Great Council Fire of the Senecas, whither, once every year, came the sachems and chiefs from the various Seneca villages to decide the weighty affairs of the nation. The kindly Colonel Johnson readily undertook fresh negotiations with Corn-Planter and in order to make sure of success, he again proceeded in person to the village at Olean Point.

His visit occurred at the most propitious of seasons, for the Indians were celebrating the Festival of the Corn when he arrived

among them. It was the one season of all the year most remarkable for general joy and happiness. Gaily was the village decked
with golden ears of corn and glowing autumn leaves while here
and there rose arbors of fresh green boughs. Men, women and
children, in gala dress, were living out-of-doors. Young men
and dusky maidens stripped the husks from off the ears with
merry laughter; here some played games of ball, tossing little
balls of deer-skin, there gaily painted warriors in the brightest
gala garments, gathered in a dance to the tom! tom! of the drum
and the shrieking of the rattle, while the squaws kept time with
awkward movements on the edges of the circle. Beneath the
fragrant pine trees old men squatted looking on, smoking their
pipes in solemn silence, and now and then grunting approval.

In the merry village, Colonel Johnson was received with all
consideration as was due to his position and long friendship with
the tribe. When he spoke of little Nelly she was summoned in
to meet him and it appeared at once that nothing had been spared
to make her garments splendid. She wore a petticoat of blue broad-
cloth, bordered with gay colored ribbons and a sack of black silk
ornamented with three rows of silver brooches. Around her neck
were strings and strings of purple wampum. Her hair was clubbed
behind and loaded with beads, her leggins were of scarlet cloth,
her moccasins of deer-skin embroidered with porcupine quills.

All the love that had been showered upon the child was evi-
denced in her garments. Nevertheless, when she had withdrawn,
Colonel Johnson, observing that the joyous festival had warmed
and opened the hearts of all, ventured to tell Corn-Planter how
the mother and father of his little sister had given up their home
and friends and come hundreds of miles to settle in a strange
land on the bare hope of sometimes looking on their loved one
or even perhaps of embracing her. Then at last the heart of
the chief was softened. There was soon to be held at Fort Nia-

gara, on the British side of the river, the Grand Council of the Senecas, and thither Corn-Planter promised to come, bringing his sister with him, that her parents might just have a glimpse of her. But he exacted a most solemn promise from Colonel Johnson that no effort should be made to reclaim the child and even that no proposal should be made to him to part with her.

Accordingly, in due time, Chief Corn-Planter set out, with Princess Nelly on horseback beside him, her heart beating with joy at thought of seeing her mother. Nelly had promised the Chief that she would never leave him without his permission, and he had perfect faith in her word.

Meantime, as the chiefs and warriors arrived in successive bands at the fort, the anxious parents watched longingly for a first sight of their daughter. At length the party was discerned emerging from the forest on the American side of the river, and Mr. and Mrs. Lytle could see at a glance that the little captive was with them. Surrounded by all the officers and ladies of the fort, they stood on the grassy bank, scarce able to contain themselves for longing impatience.

Boats were sent across by the commanding officer to fetch Corn-Planter and his party, but when they arrived the Chief alone entered one of them with his little sister. To his young men he said: "Stand here with the horses and wait until I return."

He held his darling close by the hand until the river was passed, until the boat touched the bank, then the child, no longer to be restrained, rushed forward into her mother's arms, and the two began hugging and kissing each other as though they had been fairly famished with longing.

When he beheld that sight, the great chief could withstand no longer. He spoke no word, but made an eloquent gesture of surrender. Then he turned and ordered the oarsmen to row him back alone to the farther bank. All the way over the river,

he stood in the stern of the boat, looking back with folded arms for a farewell glimpse of his loved one,—majestic, almost heroic, a noble statue in bronze, savage though he was, of sublime renunciation. No arguments nor entreaties could induce him to remain at the Council. Having gained the opposite side of the river, he called his braves about him and made off into the forest.

Mr. Lytle could scarcely believe that Corn-Planter's relinquishment of Nelly was really permanent. Dreading lest he should change his mind after a few weeks and again take steps to recover her, the father determined to change his place of abode once more. In compliance with this decision, he crossed Lake Erie with his family and settled in the neighborhood of Detroit where he continued to live thereafter.

And so it came about that little Nelly saw her good friend, the Chief, no more, but she never forgot him. Throughout all her life there remained in her heart a tender memory of the strong and forceful warrior, who had been to her as gentle as a woman.

## Hiawatha's Fasting*

*A Legend of the First Indian Corn*

HENRY WADSWORTH LONGFELLOW

You shall hear how Hi-a-wa′tha
Prayed and fasted in the forest,
Not for greater skill in hunting,
Not for greater craft in fishing,
Not for triumphs in the battle,
And renown among the warriors,
But for profit of the people,
For advantage of the nations.

    First he built a lodge for fasting,
Built a wigwam in the forest,
By the shining Big-Sea-Water.
In the blithe and pleasant Spring-time,
In the Moon of Leaves he built it,
And, with dreams and visions many,
Seven whole days and nights he fasted.

    On the first day of his fasting
Through the leafy woods he wandered;
Saw the deer start from the thicket,
Saw the rabbit in his burrow,
Heard the pheasant, Be′na, drumming,
Heard the squirrel, Ad-ji-dau′mo,
Rattling in his hoard of acorns,
Saw the pigeon, the O-me′me,
Building nests among the pine-trees,
And in flocks the wild goose, Wa′wa,
Flying to the fen-lands northward,
Whirring, wailing far above him.
"Master of Life!" he cried, desponding,
"Must our lives depend on these things?"

*Used by permission of, and by special arrangement with, Houghton Mifflin Company, the publishers.

On the next day of his fasting
By the river's brink he wandered,
Through the Musk'o-day, the meadow,
Saw the wild rice, Mah-no-mo'nee,
Saw the blueberry, Mee-nah'ga,
And the strawberry, O-dah'min,
And the grape-vine, the Be-mah'gut,
Trailing o'er the alder-branches,
Filling all the air with fragrance!
"Master of Life!" he cried, desponding,
"Must our lives depend on these things?"
On the third day of his fasting
By the lake he sat and pondered,
By the still, transparent water;
Saw the sturgeon, Nah'ma, leaping,
Scattering drops like beads of wampum,
Saw the yellow perch, the Sah'wa,
Like a sunbeam in the water,
Saw the pike, the Mask-e-no'zha,
And the Shaw'-ga-shee', the craw-fish!
"Master of Life!" he cried, desponding,
"Must our lives depend on these things?"
On the fourth day of his fasting
In his lodge he lay exhausted;
From his couch of leaves and branches
Gazing with half-open eyelids,
Full of shadowy dreams and visions,
On the dizzy, swimming landscape,
On the gleaming of the water,
On the splendor of the sunset.
And he saw a youth approaching,
Dressed in garments green and yellow,

# THE TREASURE CHEST

Coming through the purple twilight,
Through the splendor of the sunset;
Plumes of green bent o'er his forehead,
And his hair was soft and golden.
    Standing at the open doorway,
Long he looked at Hiawatha,
Looked with pity and compassion
On his wasted form and features,
And, in accents like the sighing
Of the South-Wind in the tree-tops,
Said he, "O my Hiawatha!
All your prayers are heard in heaven,
For you pray not like the others;
Not for greater skill in hunting,
Not for greater craft in fishing,
Not for triumph in the battle,
Nor renown among the warriors,
But for profit of the people,
For advantage of the nations.
    "From the Master of Life descending,
I, the friend of man, Mon-da'min,
Come to warn you and instruct you,
How by struggle and by labor
You shall gain what you have prayed for.
Rise up from your bed of branches,
Rise, O youth, and wrestle with me!"
    Faint with famine, Hiawatha
Started from his bed of branches,
From the twilight of his wigwam
Forth into the flush of sunset
Came, and wrestled with Mon-da'min;
At his touch he felt new courage,

Felt new life and hope and vigor
Run through every nerve and fibre.
   So they wrestled there together
In the glory of the sunset,
And the more they strove and struggled,
Stronger still grew Hiawatha;
Till the darkness fell around them,
And the heron, the Shuh-shuh'gah,
From her nest among the pine-trees,
Gave a cry of lamentation,
Gave a scream of pain and famine.
   " 'Tis enough!" then said Monda'min,
Smiling upon Hiawatha,
"But to-morrow, when the sun sets,
I will come again to try you."
And he vanished, and was seen not;
Whether sinking as the rain sinks,
Whether rising as the mists rise,
Hiawatha saw not, knew not,
Only saw that he had vanished,
Leaving him alone and fainting,
With the misty lake below him,
And the reeling stars above him.
   On the morrow and the next day,
When the sun through heaven descending,
Like a red and burning cinder
From the heart of the Great Spirit,
Fell into the western waters,
Came Monda'min for the trial,
For the strife with Hiawatha;
Came as silent as the dew comes,
From the empty air appearing,

384

# THE TREASURE CHEST

Into empty air returning,
Taking shape when earth it touches,
But invisible to all men
In its coming and its going.

　　Thrice they wrestled there together
In the glory of the sunset,
Till the darkness fell around them,
Till the heron, the Shuh-shuh'gah,
From her nest among the pine-trees,
Uttered her loud cry of famine,
And Monda'min paused to listen.

　　Tall and beautiful he stood there,
In his garments green and yellow;
To and fro his plumes above him
Waved and nodded with his breathing,
And the sweat of the encounter
Stood like drops of dew upon him.

And he cried, "O Hiawatha!
Bravely have you wrestled with me,
Thrice have wrestled stoutly with me,
And the Master of Life, who sees us,
He will give to you the triumph!"
Then he smiled, and said: "To-morrow
Is the last day of your conflict,
Is the last day of your fasting.
You will conquer and o'ercome me;
Make a bed for me to lie in,
Where the rain may fall upon me,
Where the sun may come and warm me;
Strip these garments, green and yellow,
Strip this nodding plumage from me,
Lay me in the earth, and make it

Soft and loose and light above me.
"Let no hand disturb my slumber,
Let no weed nor worm molest me,
Let not Kah-gah-gee', the raven,
Come to haunt me and molest me,
Only come yourself to watch me,
Till I wake, and start, and quicken,
Till I leap into the sunshine."
And thus saying, he departed;
Peacefully slept Hiawatha,
But he heard the Wa-wo-nais'sa,
Heard the whip-poor-will complaining,
Perched upon his lonely wigwam;
Heard the rushing Se-bo-wish'a,
Heard the rivulet rippling near him,
Talking to the darksome forest;
Heard the sighing of the branches,
As they lifted and subsided
At the passing of the night-wind,
Heard them, as one hears in slumber
Far-off murmurs, dreamy whispers;
Peacefully slept Hiawatha.
On the morrow came No-ko'mis,
On the seventh day of his fasting,
Came with food for Hiawatha,
Came imploring and bewailing,
Lest his hunger should o'ercome him,
Lest his fasting should be fatal.
But he tasted not, and touched not.
Only said to her, "No-ko'mis,
Wait until the sun is setting,
Till the darkness falls around us,

# THE TREASURE CHEST

Till the heron, the Shuh-shuh'gah,
Crying from the desolate marshes,
Tells us that the day is ended."
    Homeward weeping went No-ko'mis,
Sorrowing for her Hiawatha,
Fearing lest his strength should fail him,
Lest his fasting should be fatal.
He meanwhile sat weary waiting
For the coming of Monda'min,
Till the shadows, pointing eastward,
Lengthened over field and forest,
Till the sun dropped from the heaven,
As a red leaf in the Autumn
Falls and floats upon the water,
Falls and sinks into its bosom.
    And behold! the young Monda'min,
With his soft and shining tresses,
With his garments green and yellow,
With his long and glossy plumage,
Stood and beckoned at the doorway.
And as one in slumber walking,
Pale and haggard, but undaunted,
From the wigwam Hiawatha
Came and wrestled with Monda'min.
    Round about him spun the landscape,
Sky and forest reeled together,
And his strong heart leaped within him,
As the sturgeon leaps and struggles
In a net to break its meshes.
Like a ring of fire around him
Blazed and flared the red horizon,
And a hundred suns seemed looking

At the combat of the wrestlers.
　　Suddenly upon the greensward
All alone stood Hiawatha,
Panting with his wild exertion,
Palpitating with the struggle;
And before him, breathless, lifeless,
Lay the youth, with hair dishevelled,
Plumage torn, and garments tattered;
Dead he lay there in the sunset.
　　And victorious Hiawatha
Made the grave as he commanded,
Stripped the garments from Monda'min,
Stripped his tattered plumage from him,
Laid him in the earth, and made it
Soft and loose and light above him;
And the heron, the Shuh-shuh'gah,
From the melancholy moorlands,
Gave a cry of lamentation,
Gave a cry of pain and anguish.
　　Homeward then went Hiawatha
To the lodge of old Noko'mis
And the seven days of fasting
Were accomplished and completed.
But the place was not forgotten
Where he wrestled with Monda'min;
Nor forgotten nor neglected
Was the grave where lay Monda'min,
Sleeping in the rain and sunshine;
Where his scattered plumes and garments
Faded in the rain and sunshine.
　　Day by day did Hiawatha
Go to wait and watch beside it;

# THE TREASURE CHEST

Kept the dark mould soft above it,
Kept it clean from weeds and insects,
Drove away, with scoffs and shoutings,
Kah-gah-gee', the king of ravens.
　　Till at length a small green feather
From the earth shot slowly upward,
Then another and another,
And before the Summer ended
Stood the maize in all its beauty,
With its shining robes about it,
And its long, soft, yellow tresses;
And in rapture Hiawatha
Cried aloud, "It is Monda'min!
Yes, the friend of man, Monda'min!"
　　Then he called to old Noko'mis
And I-a'goo, the great boaster,
Showed them where the maize was growing,
Told them of his wondrous vision,
Of his wrestling and his triumph,
Of this new gift to the nations,
Which should be their food forever.
　　And still later, when the Autumn
Changed the long, green leaves to yellow,
And the soft and juicy kernels
Grew like wampum hard and yellow,
Then the ripened ears he gathered,
Stripped the withered husks from off them,
As he once had stripped the wrestler,
Gave the first Feast of Monda'min,
And made known unto the people
This new gift of the Great Spirit.

389

# George Rogers Clark and The Conquest of the Northwest*

THEODORE ROOSEVELT

IN 1776, when independence was declared, the United States included only the thirteen original States on the sea-board. With the exception of a few hunters there were no white men west of the Alleghany Mountains, and there was not even an American hunter in the great country out of which we have since made the States of Illinois, Indiana, Ohio, Michigan, and Wisconsin. All this region north of the Ohio River then formed a part of the Province of Quebec. It was a wilderness of forests and prairies, teeming with game, and inhabited by many warlike tribes of Indians.

Here and there through it were dotted quaint little towns of French Creoles, the most important being Detroit, Vincennes on the Wabash, and Kaskaskia and Kahokia on the Illinois. These French villages were ruled by British officers commanding small bodies of regular soldiers or Tory rangers and Creole partizans. The towns were completely in the power of the British government, none of the American States had actual possession of a foot of property in the Northwestern Territory.

The Northwest was acquired in the midst of the Revolution only by armed conquest, and if it had not been so acquired, it would have remained a part of the British Dominion of Canada.

The man to whom this conquest was due was a famous backwoods leader, a mighty hunter, a noted Indian-fighter, George Rogers Clark. He was a very strong man, with light hair and blue eyes. He was of good Virginian family. Early in his youth, he embarked on the adventurous career of a backwoods surveyor, exactly as Washington and so many other young Virginians of

Taken from *Hero Tales from American History* by the permission of the publishers, The Century Co.

spirit did at that period. He traveled out to Kentucky soon after it was founded by Boone, and lived there for a year, either at the stations or camping by himself in the woods, surveying, hunting, and making war against the Indians like any other settler, but all the time his mind was bent on vaster schemes than were dreamed of by the men around him. He had his spies out in the Northwestern Territory, and became convinced that with a small force of resolute backwoodsmen he could conquer it for the United States. When he went back to Virginia, Governor Patrick Henry entered heartily into Clark's schemes and gave him authority to fit out a force for his purpose.

In 1778, after encountering endless difficulties and delays, he finally raised a hundred and fifty backwoods riflemen. In May they started down the Ohio in flatboats to undertake the allotted task. They drifted and rowed downstream to the Falls of the Ohio, where Clark founded a log-hamlet, which has since become the great city of Louisville. Here he halted for some days and was joined by fifty or sixty volunteers, but a number of the men deserted, and when, after an eclipse of the sun, Clark again pushed off to go down with the current, his force was but about one hundred and sixty riflemen. All, however, were men on whom he could depend—men well used to frontier warfare. They were tall, stalwart backwoodsmen, clad in the hunting-shirt and leggings that formed the national dress of their kind, and armed with the distinctive weapon of the backwoods, the long-barreled, small-bore rifle.

Before reaching the Mississippi the little flotilla landed, and Clark led his men northward against the Illinois towns. In one of them, Kaskaskia, dwelt the British commander of the entire district up to Detroit. The small garrison and the Creole milita taken together outnumbered Clark's force, and they were in close alliance with the Indians roundabout. Clark was anxious to take the town by surprise and avoid bloodshed, as he believed he could win over the Creoles to the American side. Marching

cautiously by night and generally hiding by day, he came to the outskirts of the little village on the evening of July 4, and lay in the woods near by until after nightfall. Fortune favored him. That evening the officers of the garrison had given a great ball to the mirth-loving Creoles, and almost the entire population of the village had gathered in the fort, where the dance was held. While the revelry was at its height, Clark and his backwoodsmen, treading silently through the darkness, came into the town, surprised the sentries, and surrounded the fort without causing any alarm.

All the British and French capable of bearing arms were gathered in the fort to take part in or look on at the merrymaking. When his men were posted Clark walked boldly forward through the open door, and, leaning against the wall, looked at the dancers as they whirled around in the light of the flaring torches. For some moments no one noticed him. Then an Indian who had been lying with his chin on his hand, looking carefully over the gaunt figure of the stranger, sprang to his feet, and uttered the wild war-whoop. Immediately the dancing ceased and the men ran to and fro in confusion, but Clark, stepping forward, bade them be at their ease, but to remember that henceforth they danced under the flag of the United States, and not under that of Great Britain.

The surprise was complete, and no resistance was attempted. For twenty-four hours the Creoles were in abject terror. Then Clark summoned their chief men together and explained that he came as their ally, and not as their foe, and that if they would join with him they should be citizens of the American Republic, and treated in all respects on an equality with their comrades. The Creoles, caring little for the British, and rather fickle of nature, accepted the proposition with joy, and with the most enthusiastic loyalty toward Clark. Not only that, but sending messengers to their kinsmen on the Wabash, they persuaded the people of Vincennes likewise to cast off their allegiance to the British king, and to hoist the American flag.

So far, Clark had conquered with greater ease than he had dared to hope. But when the news reached the British governor, Hamilton, at Detroit, he at once prepared to reconquer the land. He had much greater forces at his command than Clark had, and in the fall of that year he came down to Vincennes by stream and portage, in a great fleet of canoes bearing five hundred fighting men—British regulars, French partisans, and Indians. The Vincennes Creoles refused to fight against the British, and the American officer who had been sent thither by Clark had no alternative but to surrender. If Hamilton had then pushed on and struck Clark in Illinois, having more than treble Clark's force, he could hardly have failed to win the victory, but the season was late and the journey so difficult that he did not believe it could be taken. Accordingly he disbanded the Indians and sent some of his troops back to Detroit, announcing that

393

when spring came he would march against Clark in Illinois.

If Clark in turn had awaited the blow he would have surely met defeat, but he was a greater man than his antagonist, and he did what the other deemed impossible.

Finding that Hamilton had sent home some of his troops and dispersed all his Indians, Clark realized that his chance was to strike before Hamilton's soldiers assembled again in the spring. Accordingly he gathered together the pick of his men, together with a few Creoles, one hundred and seventy all told, and set out for Vincennes. At first the journey was easy enough, for they passed across the snowy Illinois prairies, broken by great reaches of lofty woods. They killed elk, buffalo, and deer for food, there being no difficulty in getting all they wanted to eat, and at night they built huge fires by which to sleep, and feasted "like Indian war-dancers," as Clark said in his report.

But when, in the middle of February, they reached the drowned lands of the Wabash, where the ice had just broken up and every-thing was flooded, the difficulties seemed almost insuperable, and the march became painful and laborious to a degree. All day long the troops waded in the icy water, and at night they could with difficulty find some little hillock on which to sleep. Only Clark's indomitable courage and cheerfulness kept the party in heart and enabled them to persevere. However, persevere they did, and at last, on February 23, they came in sight of the town of Vincennes. They captured a Creole who was out shooting ducks, and from him learned that their approach was utterly unsuspected, and that there were many Indians in town.

Clark was now in some doubt as to how to make his fight. The British regulars dwelt in a small fort at one end of the town, where they had two light guns, but Clark feared lest, if he made a sudden night attack, the townspeople and Indians would, from sheer fright, turn against him. He accordingly arranged, just before he himself marched in, to send in the captured duck-hunter, conveying a warning to the Indians and the Creoles that he was about to attack the town, but that his only quarrel was with the British, and that if the other inhabitants would stay in their own homes they would not be molested.

Sending the duck-hunter ahead, Clark took up his march and entered the town just after night-fall. The news conveyed by the released hunter astounded the townspeople, and they talked it over eagerly, and were in doubt what to do. The Indians, not knowing how great might be the force that would assail the town, at once took refuge in the neighboring woods, while the Creoles retired to their own houses. The British knew nothing of what had happened until the Americans had actually entered the streets of the little village. Rushing forward, Clark's men soon penned the regulars within their fort, where they kept them surrounded all night. The next day a party of Indian warriors, who in the British interest had been ravaging the settlements of Kentucky, arrived and entered the town, ignorant that the Americans had captured it. Marching boldly forward to the fort, they suddenly found it beleaguered, and before they could flee they were seized by the backwoodsmen. In their belts they carried the scalps of the slain settlers. The savages were taken redhanded, and the American frontiersmen were in no mood to show mercy. All the Indians were tomahawked in sight of the fort.

For some time the British defended themselves well, but at length their guns were disabled, all of the gunners being picked off by the backwoods marksmen, and finally the garrison dared not so much as appear at a port-hole, so deadly was the fire from the long rifles. Under such circumstances Hamilton was forced to surrender. No attempt was afterward made to molest the Americans in the land they had won, and upon the conclusion of peace the Northwest, which had been conquered by Clark, became part of the United States.

## The Boyhood of Robert Fulton

 DILLAR, a dollar, a ten o'clock scholar—that was what Robert Fulton was on the day that he stood, self-conscious and apologetic, before the austere old Quaker schoolmaster, Caleb Johnson, in the little town of Lancaster, Pennsylvania. An important personage was the schoolmaster of those days—the early days of the American Revolution,—and Caleb grasped his birch rod sternly as he peered over his huge rimmed spectacles at the little truant before him.

"Robert Fulton!" he cried. "Why does thee come so late? Wasting thy time on the streets, I suppose, in idle dilly-dallying! Thee will grow up a lazy, empty-headed good-for-naught!" And he held his birch rod in a state of unpleasant preparation for immediate and summary vengeance. The boy's cheeks glowed.

"Nay!" he cried eagerly. "I am late I know and I am sorry but I have not been lazy nor idle. I have spent the time at Nicholas Miller's shop making somewhat of which I had need!" And he held up to the astonished schoolmaster a perfectly turned lead pencil in a day when lead pencils were not the easily procured article that they have been in later years. "I pounded out the lead, made the wooden case and fitted the lead into it all myself," went on the boy, "and when I'm at tasks like that I forget how time is passing."

The children looked up from their books open-mouthed with wonder and old Caleb himself could not repress a sudden gleam of interest. It was indeed a remarkably well-made pencil. Beneath his crusty exterior the schoolmaster had a heart by no means lacking in warmth, and he secretly felt more than a little interest in this strange pupil of his. It was true Robert's thoughts all too frequently wandered from his studies, yet on such occasions it almost invariably proved that, far from being idle, he had been solving some knotty problem, originating some wonderful idea how he could make this or that marvelous contrivance to meet some need of his own, his mother's or his friends'. So, though Caleb's dignity still demanded that he mutter something beneath his breath, shake his head and finger his birch-rod threateningly as he motioned the culprit to take his seat, he said to himself in secret that the world would yet hear from that original little urchin who had just excaped a trouncing.

Robert Fulton was indeed the most original boy of his time in the little town of Lancaster. He seemed invariably able to supply his own wants, no matter how strange they were, by most remarkable articles of his own design and construction. As he grew somewhat older, two absorbing interests claimed his life,— the study of machinery and the study of art. For with that lead pencil which he had so carefully turned in Nicholas Miller's shop he soon began to draw. He drew sign-boards for the inns of the town to earn money for his support; but what interested him still more, he sketched parts of machinery in the various shops of the village and made himself so useful to the mechanics that they always welcomed his visits. Indeed he used to draw plans and designs for all sorts of things which he himself wished to construct, and while he was not always prepared to recite in

Master Caleb Johnson's school on the particular lesson for the day, he read and studied greedily both in school and out all the books he could find on matters that interested him, — mathematics, chemistry, mechanics and all related subjects.

On the approach of the Fourth of July, 1778, when Robert was

thirteen years old, the boys of Lancaster planned a wonderful celebration in honor of the second anniversary of the Declaration of Independence. The war was still in hot progress and their bubbling boyish devotion to the cause of liberty was in direst need of a safety valve in order to let off steam. So they had planned to illuminate the city splendidly with candles. On the first day of July, however, the city council, gravely discussing the necessity for pressing economy in such trying times, and most particularly taking into consideration the great scarcity of tallow, issued solemn orders that no lighting of candles should be permitted to celebrate the Fourth.

A sad blow indeed to the boys! They stood before the signboard announcing this sorry injunction, with their hands in their pockets and their faces long and sober. Robert Fulton alone wasted no time in regrets. He stood for a few moments lost in thought. Then home he went and buried himself for a time in a book. Afterward he hurried away to the brush maker's and exchanged the candles he had been saving for gun powder. At a second shop near by, he bought some sheets of cardboard, and the clerk in this latter shop felt a flash of curiosity as he handed the boy his purchase.

"What are you going to do with that cardboard?" he asked.

The boy answered eagerly: "We are forbidden to light the streets with candles, so I'm going to light the sky with rockets!"

The man laughed heartily as though the words were a joke. Fire works were then practically unknown in Europe and America, though they had long been used in China.

"Light the sky!" he chuckled. "Why, that's impossible."

The boy flung back his head with an air of positive certainty.

"Impossible!" he cried. "No sir! There is nothing impossible!"

And sure enough! When the great night came, and the sun sank down into the tops of the trees beyond the Conestoga

River, the boys gathered in the center of the city square and built a gigantic bon-fire. When the leaping of the flames and the shouts of the lads had drawn to the place all the people of Lancaster, the youngsters turned to a row of cardboard cylinders attached to sticks that were lying on the grass at a safe distance from the blaze. Under Robert's direction they had made these cylinders, and it had required the greatest care and mathematical accuracy to have them of exactly the proper length and thickness, and the stick exactly the proper length in proportion to the size of the cylinders. The head of the rocket was filled with powder and a number of little balls, most carefully compounded by Robert himself and consisting of various ingredients to make colored fire. All this—the compounding of materials, the proper dimensions and proportions—Robert had carefully studied out from the general description which he had read in his book.

When the boys set off the rockets, "Oh" and "Ah!" cried tne astonished crowd. A big report, then a streak of fire shooting up like a hissing dragon into the air and finally high above their heads a burst of glorious colored stars.

The citizens of Lancaster had no words but of praise that night for the intelligent little lad who had worked out for them such a celebration and the boys themselves felt that rockets far outdid candles as a means of venting youthful spirits.

After this Robert continued more constantly than ever to haunt the factories where arms were being made for the Continental army, and he proved so good a draughtsman, such a student of mechanics and of such an inventive turn of mind, that he was often able to give the workmen valuable suggestions. Always and eternally he was experimenting, experimenting, experimenting. Sometimes he worked quite mysteriously on problems he would not discuss with his fellows. Once he continued day after day to go to the druggist's for quicksilver. Great was the curiosity to know what he could be doing with that strange elusive metal that acts as if bewitched. No one ever discovered; he kept it a deep, dark secret, but his comrades thenceforth nicknamed him "Quicksilver Bob."

In 1779 when he was fourteen years old, Quicksilver Bob met among the factory youths an intelligent lad four years older than he who rejoiced in the name of Christopher Gumpf. Now the father of Christopher was an enthusiastic fisherman and he kept an old flat boat padlocked to a tree on the banks of the Conestoga. Often he would invite the boys to go with him on fishing trips up the river. On holidays they would all three set out with bait and lunch for a glorious day up stream. The flat boat was propelled by a pole, and the boys took turns at poling. But it was a hard and tedious task pushing the clumsy, heavy old scow for a long distance up stream, so then and there Robert's active mind began to work on the problem of saving labor in locomotion by water. During a visit of a week with an aunt in New Britain, he planned and made a small model of a boat to be propelled by side paddles. The model was too large to be carried home, so Robert on his departure left it in his aunt's attic. Little did she guess that day that in after years it should be her most cherished treasure.

# THE TREASURE CHEST

On returning to Lancaster, Fulton confided his plan for moving a boat by paddle wheels to Christopher. After much secret hammering, sawing and planing in the woods by the river, the two lads together made a set of side paddles to move their old friend, the scow. The paddle wheels were joined by a bar and worked by a crank, so that one boy, standing in the center of the boat could turn the crank, which would turn the bar, which would turn the paddle wheels, which would propel the boat!

When the contrivance was finished Christopher himself could hardly believe it would work, but Robert, with no doubts whatever, stepped into the boat, confidently laid hold of the crank and turned it with a vim. Off went the scow, gliding along upstream, and the boys spent a day of delighted triumph, enjoying their success and the astonished faces of the spectators who stopped, open mouthed, to watch them from the banks of the Conestoga. Very little effort now sent the boat a long way. It was much easier and faster than the old fashioned method of poling.

So it was in the little town of Lancaster on the Conestoga Creek, with only a few witnesses who little dreamed what the contrivance would lead to, that the boy, Robert Fulton, began to plan his solution to the problem of navigation. Years later, in place of a few astonished rustics lining a creek to see a paddle-wheeled scow, crowds of people were to line the banks of the Hudson to see the Clermont, the first successful steamboat ever launched, steam its way up the river, puffing out its message to all the world that it brought an end to the days of sail-boats and ushered in the dawn of the era of steam navigation. And the inventor of the Clermont, the boat that revolutionized the method of travel by water, was this same Robert Fulton, who had proclaimed as a boy with all simple but fervent sincerity, that to him who has courage and purpose, patience and faith, "nothing is impossible."

## Gideon, the Warrior
### Judges VI:1–16, 33–40, VII, VIII:22, 23, 28

And the children of Israel did evil in the sight of the Lord; and the Lord delivered them into the hand of Mid′i-an seven years. And the hand of Mid′i-an prevailed against Israel; and because of the Mid′i-an-ites, the children of Israel made them the dens which are in the mountains, and caves, and strongholds.

And so it was that the Mid′i-an-ites came up, and the Am-a′-lek-ites, and the children of the East, and they encamped against the children of Israel, and destroyed the increase of the earth, and left no sustenance for Israel, neither sheep, nor ox, nor ass. For they came up with their cattle and their tents, and they came as grasshoppers for multitude; for they and their camels were without number, and they entered into the land to destroy it.

# THE TREASURE CHEST

And Israel was greatly impoverished because of the Mid'i-an-ites; and the children of Israel cried unto the Lord. And it came to pass when the children of Israel cried unto the Lord, that the Lord sent a prophet unto the children of Israel, which said unto them:

"Thus saith the Lord God of Israel, 'I brought you up from Egypt, and brought you forth out of the land of bondage; and I delivered you out of the hand of the Egyptians, and out of the hand of all that oppressed you, and drave them out from before you and gave you their land.' And I said unto you, 'I am the Lord your God; fear not the gods of the Am'or-ites, in whose land you dwell. But ye have not obeyed my voice.'"

And there came an angel of the Lord, and sat under an oak which was in Oph'rah, that pertained unto Jo'ash, the A'bi-ez'rite. And his son Gid'e-on threshed wheat by the winepress, to hide it from the Midianites. And the angel of the Lord appeared unto him, and said unto him, "The Lord is with thee, thou mighty man of valor."

And Gideon said unto him, "Oh, my Lord, if the Lord be with us, why then is all this befallen us? And where be all his miracles, which our fathers told us of, saying, 'Did not the Lord bring us up from Egypt?' But now the Lord hath forsaken us, and delivered us into the hands of the Midianites."

And the Lord looked upon him and said, "Go in this thy might, and thou shalt save Israel from the hands of the Midianites. Have not I sent thee?"

And Gideon said unto him: "Oh, my Lord, wherewith shall I save Israel? Behold my family is poor in Ma-nas'seh, and I am the least in my father's house."

And the Lord said unto him: "Surely I will be with thee, and thou shalt smite the Midianites as one man."

Then all the Midianites and the Amalekites and the children of the East were gathered together and pitched in the valley of Jez're-el. But the Spirit of the Lord came upon Gideon, and he blew a trumpet; and A'bi-e'zer was gathered after him; and he sent messengers throughout all Ma-nas'seh; who also were gathered after him, and he sent messengers unto Ash'er, and unto Zeb'u-lun, and unto Naph'ta-li; and they came up to meet them.

And Gideon said unto God: "If thou wilt save Israel by mine hand, as thou has said, behold! I will put a fleece of wool on the floor, and if the dew be on the fleece only, and it be dry upon all the earth beside, then shall I know that thou wilt save Israel by mine hand, as thou hast said."

And it was so, for he rose up early on the morrow, and wringed the dew out of the fleece, a bowl full of water.

And Gideon said unto God: "Let not thine anger be hot against me, and I will speak but this once: let me prove, I pray thee, but this once with the fleece. Let it now be dry upon the fleece, and upon all the ground let there be dew."

And God did so that night; for it was dry upon the fleece only, and there was dew on all the ground.

Then Gideon, and all the people that were with him, rose up early, and pitched beside the well of Ha'rod; so that the host of the Midianites were on the north side of them, by the hill of Mo'reh, in the valley.

And the Lord said unto Gideon: "The people that are with thee are too many for me to give the Midianites into their hands, lest Israel vaunt themselves against me, saying, 'Mine *own* hand hath saved me.' Now therefore, go to; proclaim in the ears of the people saying, 'Whosoever is fearful and afraid, let him return and depart early from Mount Gil'e-ad.' "

And there returned of the people twenty and two thousand, and there remained ten thousand.

And the Lord said unto Gideon: "The people are yet too many. Bring them down unto the water and I will try them for thee there. And it shall be that of whom I say unto thee, 'This shall go with thee,' the same shall go with thee; and of whomsoever I say unto thee, 'The same shall not go with thee,' the same shall not go."

So he brought down the people unto the water, and the Lord said unto Gideon: "Every one that lappeth of the water with his tongue, as a dog lappeth, him shalt thou set by himself; likewise everyone that boweth down upon his knees to drink."

And the number of them that lapped, putting their hand to their mouth, were three hundred men. But all the rest of the people bowed down upon their knees to drink water.

And the Lord said unto Gideon: "By the three hundred men that lapped will I save you, and deliver the Midianites into thine hand. Let all the other people go, every man unto his place."

So the people took victuals in their hand, and their trumpets, and he sent all the rest of Israel every man unto his tent, and retained but those three hundred men only. And the host of Midian was beneath him in the valley.

And it came to pass the same night, that the Lord said unto him: "Arise, get thee down unto the host; for I have delivered it into thine hand. But if thou fear to go down, go thou with Phu'rah thy servant down to the host. And thou shalt hear what they say, and afterward shall thine hand be strengthened to go down against the host."

Then went he down with Phurah his servant unto the outside

of the armed men that were in the host. And the Midianites, and the Amalekites and all the children of the East lay along in the valley like grasshoppers for multitude; and their camels were without number, as the sand by the seaside for multitude.

And when Gideon was come, behold! there was a man that told a dream unto his fellow, and said: "Behold! I dreamed a dream, and lo! a cake of barley bread tumbled into the host of Midian, and came unto a tent and smote it that it fell, and overturned it that the tent lay along."

And his fellow answered and said: "This is nothing else save the sword of Gideon, the son of Joash, a man of Israel; for into his hand hath God delivered Midian and all the host."

And it was so when Gideon heard the telling of the dream, and the interpretation thereof, that he worshipped and returned unto the host of Israel and said: "Arise, for the Lord hath delivered into your hand the host of Midian."

And he divided the three hundred men into three companies, and he put a trumpet in every man's hand, with empty pitchers, and torches within the pitchers. And he said unto them: "Look on me and do likewise. And behold! when I come to the outside of the camp, it shall be that, as I do, so shall ye do. When I blow a trumpet, I and all that are with me, then blow ye the trumpets also on every side of all the camp, and say, *'The Sword of the Lord and of Gideon!'* "

So Gideon and the hundred men that were with him came unto the outside of the camp in the beginning of the middle watch, and they had but newly set the watch. And they blew the trumpets and brake the pitchers that were in their hands. And the three companies blew the trumpets, and brake the pitchers that were in their hands, and held the torches in their left hands, and the trumpets in their right hands to blow withal. And they cried, "*The Sword of the Lord and of Gideon!*"

And they stood every man in his place round about the camp, and the Midianites thought an host was come upon them and they ran and the children of Israel shouted and put them to flight. And the three hundred blew the trumpets and the Lord set every man's sword against his fellow, even throughout all the host of Midian, and the Midianites fled. And the men of Israel gathered themselves together and pursued after the Midianites.

Then the men of Israel said unto Gideon: "Rule thou over us, both thou and thy son, and thy son's son also, for thou hast delivered us from the hand of Midian."

And Gideon said unto them: "I will not rule over you, neither shall my son rule over you; the Lord shall rule over you."

Thus was Midian subdued before the children of Israel, so that they lifted up their heads no more. And the country was in quietness forty years in the days of Gideon.

## Daniel in the Lions' Den
### Daniel, 6.

It pleased King Da-ri′us to set over the kingdom of Bab′y-lon an hundred and twenty princes which should be over the whole kingdom; and over these three presidents, of whom that Daniel who was of the captives of Judah, was first, that the princes might give accounts unto the presidents, and the king should have no damage. Then this Daniel was preferred above the presidents and princes because an excellent spirit was in him, and the King thought to set him over the whole realm.

Then the presidents and princes sought to find occasion against Daniel concerning the kingdom. But they could find none occasion nor fault, forasmuch as he was faithful, neither was there any error or fault found in him.

Then said these men, "We shall not find any occasion against this Daniel, except we find it against him concerning the law of his God."

Then these presidents and princes assembled together to the King and said thus unto him:

"King Darius, live forever! All the presidents of the King-dom, the governors and the princes, the counsellors and the captains, have consulted together to establish a royal statute and to make a firm decree, that whosoever shall ask a petition of any God or man for thirty days, save of thee, O King, he shall be cast into the den of lions. Now, O King, establish the decree, and sign the writing, that it be not changed, according to the law of the Medes and Persians, which altereth not."

Wherefore King Darius signed the writing and the decree.

Now when Daniel knew that the writing was signed, he went into his house; and his windows being opened in his chamber toward Jerusalem, he kneeled upon his knees three times a day, and prayed and gave thanks before his God as he did aforetime.

Then these men assembled, and found Daniel praying and making supplication before his God. Then they came near, and spake before the King concerning the King's decree:

"Hast thou not signed a decree that every man that shall ask a petition of any God or man within thirty days, save of thee, O King, shall be cast into the den of lions?"

The King answered and said:

"The thing is true according to the law of the Medes and Persians which altereth not."

Then answered they and said before the King:

"That Daniel which is of the children of the captivity of Judah regardeth not thee, O King, nor the decree that thou hast signed, but maketh his petition three times a day."

Then the King, when he heard these words, was sore displeased with himself, and set his heart on Daniel to deliver him. And he labored till the going down of the sun to deliver him.

Then these men assembled unto the King and said unto the King:

"Know, O King, that the law of the Medes and Persians is that no decree or statute which the King establisheth may be changed."

Then the King commanded and they brought Daniel and cast him into the den of lions. Now the King spake and said unto Daniel:

"Thy God whom thou servest continually, he will deliver thee."

And a stone was brought and laid upon the mouth of the den, and the King sealed it with his own signet, and with the signet of his lords; that the purpose might not be changed concerning Daniel.

Then the King went to his palace, and passed the night fasting; neither were instruments of music brought before him, and his sleep went from him.

Then the King arose very early in the morning, and went in haste unto the den of lions. And when he came to the den, he cried with a lamentable voice unto Daniel. And the King spake and said to Daniel:

"O Daniel, servant of the living God, is thy God whom thou servest continually able to deliver thee from the lions?"

Then said Daniel unto the King:

"O King, live forever! My God hath sent his angel, and hath shut the lions' mouths, that they have not hurt me; forasmuch as before him innocency was found in me; and also before thee, O King, have I done no hurt."

Then was the King exceeding glad for him, and commanded that they should take Daniel up out of the den. So Daniel was taken up out of the den, and no manner of hurt was found upon him, because he believed in his God.

And the King commanded and they brought those men which had

accused Daniel, and they cast *them* into the den of lions; and the lions had the mastery of them.

Then King Darius wrote unto all peoples, nations and languages, that dwell in all the earth:

"Peace be multiplied unto you! I make a decree, that in every dominion of my kingdom, men tremble and fear before the God of Daniel; for he is the living God, and steadfast forever, and his kingdom that which shall not be destroyed, and his dominion shall be even unto the end. He delivereth and rescueth, and he worketh signs and wonders in heaven and in earth, who hath delivered Daniel from the power of the lions."

So this Daniel prospered in the reign of Darius, and in the reign of Cyrus, the Persian.

## The Adventures of Perseus

### A Greek Myth

HERE dwelt once in Argos, a King's daughter named Dan'a-e and her infant son, Per'se-us. Now Ac-ris'i-us, the father of Danae, had one day been terrified half out of his wits by the words of an oracle which solemnly declared that the child of his daughter, Danae, should be the cause of his death. Thereafter, blindly accepting the words of the oracle as true, and heeding naught but his own foolish fears, Acrisius caused Danae and her son to be seized out of the strong tower wherein he had confined them, shut fast in an iron-bound chest, and cast into the sea.

Up and down on the boundless deep rocked the chest, now borne high aloft on the crest of a giant wave, and now plunged headlong down into the foaming trough of the sea. Within, Danae held close her babe, and prayed to be delivered. Out and out they drifted, far and far and far. At last the waters heaved them up onto the shore of an island, and the chest was entangled fast in a fisherman's net.

Now the fisherman was amazed when he drew up out of the sea an iron-bound box, and found it to contain a young mother and child of marvelous beauty. Straightway he led them to his own cottage and commended them to the care of his wife. It then appeared that the name of the island, whereon they had been cast, was Ser'i-phus, and the fisherman was Dic'tys, no less a personage than brother to King Pol-y-dec'tes himself. In the cottage of Dictys and his good wife, Danae and her son were sheltered till Perseus grew to manhood.

Then it chanced one day that Polydectes cast his eyes on Danae and determined to have her for his queen. But Danae would have none of Polydectes, for he was a tyrant both wicked and cruel. By this time Perseus was grown a youth of such strength and promise that he was well able to defend his mother, and Polydectes perceived that if he would worry the lovely Danae into becoming his bride, he must rid himself of her stalwart son. Therefore he called to him the young Perseus and said:

"Youth, you have found in my kingdom an asylum and a home from the days of your infancy. Now that you are grown to manhood, it is but meet that you should repay the courtesy thus extended to you. You have reached the age when men of valor go venturing, to rid the world of monsters. Go you, therefore, in quest of the gorgon, Med-u'sa, who lays waste all the surrounding countryside, and show your face no more within my kingdom until you bring to me her head."

Now Perseus withdrew from the presence of King Polydectes almost in despair. He would have shrunk from no ordinary adventure possible to a hero, but the gorgons, as he knew full well, were the most hideous monsters in the world. Three terrible sisters they were, hateful, venomous, cruel. They had faces like women, but their bodies were those of beasts, all covered with scales of brass and iron so hard that no sword could pierce them; enormous were their wings and they gleamed with sinister flash of golden feathers; they had tusks instead of teeth, and sharp, cruel, brazen claws. Their hair was writhing serpents, that would curl and twist and hiss, and dart out long, forked tongues to sting. Worst of all, so hard and cold and hateful was their stare, that he who looked full in their faces froze immediately into stone.

"Now how," mused Perseus, "is a man to give battle to such horrid creatures when he may not even look on them?"

Nevertheless, he bade a sad farewell to his mother, and wandered along the shore lost in sorrowful thoughts and longing for some wise counsel. Suddenly there glowed about him a light seven times brighter than the sun. He looked up in amazement

and lo! there before him, resting lightly on the sand, stood a beautiful woman in long white robes with a shining helmet on her head, a staff in her hand, and a shield on her arm,—Min-er'va, the goddess of Wisdom herself.

"Perseus," said she, "take this shield. So brightly is it polished that if you keep your eyes fixed upon it, you will see the gorgons reflected therein, and can give them battle without ever needing to look in their faces."

With a mighty leaping of his heart, Perseus gave thanks, yet he said: "Though I look in the shield, where shall I find among mortals a sword that can pierce through their heavy scales?"

Even as he spoke, there came a slight rustling through the air, and hovering there on his other side appeared a youth with winged sandals and cap, in one hand a winged staff, about which two serpents were twined, and in the other a crooked sword that shone like a flame.

"You shall use my sword," said the youth, for he was Mer'-cu-ry, messenger from O-lymp'us whence came the help of the gods to men who had deserved it.

# THE TREASURE CHEST

Then Minerva bade the young Perseus seek out the Three Gray Sisters, cousins of the gorgons, and force from them the secret of where the Gorgons' Isle lay. Guided by Mercury, Perseus made off.

Far, far to westward he journeyed, till he came to a barren desolate shore, where was everlasting twilight. Gray was the sky, and gray were the giant rocks; gray were the straggling trunks of the leafless trees, and gray was the misty sea. As the two approached the place, there loomed up before them three old hags in flowing gray robes with unkempt white locks hanging over their shoulders, scarce to be told from the great gray waves with crests of white that came dashing up on the shore. Perseus perceived that these three old hags possessed but one tooth and one eye among them. These they passed about from one to another and each in turn clapped the tooth into her toothless gums, and the eye into a socket in her forehead. As Perseus and Mercury groped their way cautiously towards them, it became apparent

that the old hags were just at that moment quarreling over whose turn it was to have the eye. One held the brilliant orb gleaming in her hand, and all were scolding, gesticulating, screeching. Thus, the while they wrangled, not one of the three could see at all.

"Quick," whispered Mercury to Perseus. "Now is your chance. Seize the eye and do not return it till they tell you the secret. They will never tell you otherwise."

In a flash Perseus stepped

forward, nimbly seized the eye, and withdrew again to a little distance. Then there burst forth a perfect storm from the three old hags, for each thought the other had snatched the eye, but Perseus cried out boldly:

"I have your eye,—I, a youth from beyond the seas, nor will I return it until you tell me where lies the Island of the Gorgons."

The old hags begged and whined and scolded; they tried to grope their way stealthily to him to snatch back the eye unawares, but Perseus kept well out of reach and held firm. So at last they told him that he must go still farther westward, and there seek out certain nymphs who kept a pair of winged sandals, a magic pouch and a wonderful helmet that could render its wearer invisible. These nymphs would direct him just how to reach the Island of the Gorgons.

At that Perseus gave the Gray Women back their eye, and with Mercury journeyed once more forward. In good time, they reached a beautiful glade in the forest, where the sunlight filtered in blotches of gold through the leaves, and a group of graceful nymphs with wreaths and garlands of flowers, disported themselves about the banks of a clear, blue pool. To them Perseus presented himself and told his tale. At once they hushed their mirth and musical laughter.

"We will gladly aid the hero who goes forth to conquer the gorgon, Medusa," they cried, and they tripped lightly away, brought back the winged sandals and bound them on Perseus' feet. About his neck they hung the magic pouch, and placed on his head the helmet of darkness. When they had thus provided him, they pointed out the Island of the Gorgons lying low, like a bank of dun gray clouds, on the dim horizon.

Now in his winged sandals Perseus could mount up into the air as safely as Mercury. Far, far up he soared, cleaving the air like a bird, now skimming over the chequered green earth that lay spread out far below, and now over the shining blue sea. It was midnight when Perseus at length heard a calm voice speak by his side, grave, yet melodious and mild.

"There below," it said, "lies the Island of the Gorgons." And now it was not Mercury who spoke, but Minerva, come once more in the hour of need to give Perseus counsel. Wrapped from sight in the helmet of darkness, Perseus sank downward. The moon was flooding the earth with silver, and he saw below him a rocky coast, stone, stone, everywhere stone, shining white and cold in the cold, white light. Suddenly from among the black shadows at the base of a barren cliff, there flashed a baleful gleam, and he knew it must be a moonbeam cast back from the horrid scales on the backs of the gorgons. Boldly he descended thither.

"Be cautious," said Minerva, "look into your shield."

Then in the full-glowing light of the moon, he looked into his shield and behold! a hideous sight,— the three hateful sisters fast asleep, their scales and golden wings glistening, their brazen claws outspread as though ready to clutch, the snakes on their heads writhing even in sleep, and hissing now and again. Even as he looked, one of the dreadful creatures moved as though to awake.

"That is Medusa," said Minerva, "strike on the instant and do not miss your first stroke."

In a flash Perseus obeyed. The gorgon opened her freezing eyes, but Perseus, looking ever into the shield, cleaved off the

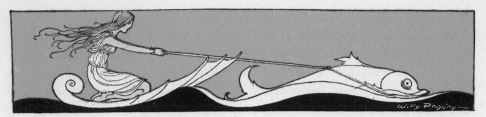

head with a single stroke of his sword, seized it, snakes and all, and dropped it into the magic pouch.

"Well done," cried Mercury.

"Now fly," said Minerva, "for the others are awakening."

On his winged sandals, Perseus sped swiftly upward, but not a moment too soon. Medusa's sisters, awakened by the noise of his stroke, perceived what had been done, and flew in a frenzy of rage to the shore, every snake on their heads a-bristle with fury. He could hear the rushing of their wings, the rattle of their brazen claws, the hissing of the serpents, as they mounted up into the air in pursuit. But, thanks to the helmet of darkness, he was hidden from their sight, and made off from them in safety.

Perseus then bade farewell to Mercury and Minerva, and set out alone to return to Seriphus. But it chanced on the way that he passed through the country of E-thi-o'pi-a, which was ruled over by King Ceph'e-us. Now there was come up at this time out of the deep a terrible sea monster, that ravaged the coast of Ethiopia, a huge, scaly creature with wings like a dragon and a tail like a fish. It came up and carried off oxen and people, and even destroyed whole villages. The men of Ethiopia had done all in their power to rid themselves of the monster, but in vain,—there was not one among them able to stand before him. Then came forward a wise old man of the people and said:

"Lo! our queen, Cass-i-o-pe'i-a, swelled with pride of her own beauty, did boast herself lovelier than the sea-nymphs, that drive their chariots with swift-skimming dolphins through the waves.

# THE TREASURE CHEST

This frightful monster is come up out of the sea as a punishment to her vanity, and never will he retire till the guilty queen offer to him her dearest treasure, even An-drom'e-da, her daughter."

Throughout all the kingdom, then, was weeping and wailing, and most of all in the palace. Nevertheless, the people must at all costs be rid of the monster, so they seized the lovely Andromeda, bound her fast with chains to a mighty rock on the shore and left her a prey to the beast. Andromeda wrung her hands; the people stood afar off and watched, but they dared not let her free. Even Phin'e-us, whose promised bride she was, stood by and made no effort to save her. Pale and motionless as a marble statue, save for her hair that waved in the breeze, she stood.

Then lo! up out of the sea like a mountain he rose,—the great sea-monster! Andromeda shrieked; the wretched mother and father wrung their hands; Phineus shrank back, slunk away, and hid himself in fear. But there in that moment of despair, borne

419

up in the air by his winged sandals, appeared the hero, Perseus.

"O virgin," he cried, "undeserving those chains. I am come to deliver you."

With a sudden swoop the youth darted down on the back of the monster, lighting just at the base of the neck where the creature could not strike at him with his fangs. Into his shoulder Perseus plunged his sword. Now here, now there, he worried him, piercing first this side, then that, and darting ever out of his reach by means of his wings. With a furious splashing the monster churned all the water about into foam. At length Perseus' wings were drenched. He dared no longer trust them. Alighting now on a rock and holding fast to a projecting fragment, as the monster floated near, he gave him his death blow. The serpent turned over on his back and floated with belly upward.

The people, gathered on the shore, raised a shout till all the hills re-echoed. The parents, transported with joy, called Perseus their deliverer, and the hero himself released Andromeda from the rocks. Then was the lovely Andromeda promised to Perseus in marriage. Every house in the city was wreathed and hung with garlands. In the palace itself a banquet was spread and all was joy and festivity.

But suddenly a noise was heard of warlike clamor. With a numerous party of swaggering, brawling followers, there burst into the festal hall, Phineus, demanding the maiden as his own. It was in vain that Cepheus cried: "You should have claimed her when she lay bound to the rock, the monster's victim. He who neglects his claim at such a time, forfeits it altogether."

Phineus made no reply, but hurled his javelin at Perseus. It missed its mark and fell harmless. Then the cowardly assailant ran and took shelter behind the altar. His act was the signal for a general onset by his band upon the guests of Cepheus. Perseus and his friends defended themselves and maintained for some time the unequal conflict, but the numbers of the assailants were far too great. Destruction seemed inevitable. Then with a loud voice Perseus cried: "If I have any friend here, let him turn away his eyes." And he suddenly held aloft the head of the gorgon, Medusa.

"Seek not to frighten us with your jugglery," cried one of the brawlers and raised his javelin to throw, but lo! he was turned to stone in the very act. A second was about to plunge his sword into a prostrate foe, but his arm stiffened and he could thrust not a hairsbreadth forward. A third, in the midst of a taunting boast, froze with mouth wide open. Phineus, beholding the dreadful result of his unjust aggression, felt confounded. He called aloud to his friends and got no answer. He touched them and found them stone. Then he fell on his knees before Perseus, to sue for his own wretched life, but in the very attitude he, too, was turned to stone.

Then was the marriage of Perseus and Andromeda fulfilled. King Cepheus gave Perseus a ship with stalwart rowers; he and his queen bade a fond farewell to their daughter, Andromeda, and Perseus and his bride set out for Seriphus.

Now it had happened that while Perseus had been away on his adventures, Polydectes had never once left off worrying Danae to force her to be his queen. His followers were as wicked as he, and in all the island was none to protect the lovely young matron, save Dictys, the good fisherman. At last, in his anger, the King cast Danae and Dictys both into dungeons, and there the two lay languishing when the ship of Perseus dropped anchor in the harbor.

Perseus made straight for the palace. The King was at meat surrounded by his wicked retainers. When he saw come into the hall the youth whom he had thought out of his way forever, he was sunk at first in confusion. In a moment more he cried out:

"How dare you come here without the head of Medusa?"

"O King," Perseus answered, "I have the head in my pouch."

"Ho, ho!" mocked the King, "if you have in truth performed this unheard-of-act, then show us the head."

"Nay," answered Perseus. "I am loath to hold it up. I tell you I have it here in my pouch."

"Ho! ho!" jeered all the King's followers. "He has it in his pouch, yet he will not produce it! Base deceiver, he but pretends to have done the deed. It is no Medusa head he has in his pouch. He dares not show us what lies there."

"Come, come," called the King, "if you have there the head, out with it on the instant! Else with your own head you shall pay for the cheat."

Threatening, taunting, gibing, the King's men pressed about Perseus. "As you will, then," shouted the hero, and he held it aloft,—the snaky head of Medusa. In a flash, about him were a white marble hall, a white marble table with white marble food and marble statues of men.

Having thus freed the island from the base tyranny of Polydectes, Perseus went to embrace his mother, set her free, and lead her to his Andromeda. Dictys likewise he freed and made King of Seriphus in place of his worthless brother. To Minerva Perseus returned her shield along with the gift of the head of Medusa. To Mercury he gave back the sword. Then Perseus and Andromeda, with Danae, their mother, once more sailed away and after many adventures Perseus found a kingdom for himself. Long and wisely he reigned, and lived happily thenceforward.

## The Labors of Hercules
### A Greek Myth

Among all the Greek heroes about whom the old Greek harpers sung, who was more dearly loved than Her'cu-les—Hercules, the patient, Hercules the strong?

When Hercules was but a babe a few months old, his mother, Alc-me'ne, left him once asleep in a brazen warrior's shield that served him for a cradle. There came creeping upon him while he slept, two venomous serpents. Just as the snakes were about to strike, Hercules awoke. With a crow of delight, as though he had found a new plaything, and without a sign of fear, the little one seized the serpents, one in each hand. Straight by the neck he grasped them and held on tight. When his mother came in and found him thus, she was struck almost dumb at the sight, but the snakes were already strangled, and the infant Hercules safe. So began the strong man's conquests over evil.

Hercules grew to manhood possessed of marvelous courage and strength and carefully trained in all that befitted a hero. One day when he was still a youth, dwelling for a time among herdsmen on the mountains, he lay down in a lonely valley to sleep through the noonday heat. In his sleep he had a strange dream. He seemed to be following a path that suddenly split into two, branching off in opposite directions, and he knew not which road to take in order to pursue his journey. One road looked broad and easy and led down to a pleasant city whence he saw the gleam of marble palaces mid green and tempting gardens. The other was steep and rocky. It was hard to climb and led endlessly upward, growing rockier and rougher at every step, till it disappeared in the clouds. As Hercules stood hesitating which road to choose, there came dancing down the smooth and easy highway a gay and laughing maiden. She beckoned to him and called:

"Come with me, Hercules, down into the pleasant city. There you need not labor all day long in the heat of the sun. You may sit continually in fragrant gardens, hearken to the splash of fountains and the songs of birds, and slaves will serve you with all you need."

As Hercules looked toward the city, the piping of merry music faintly reached his ears to invite and tempt him still further. But lo! just then in the second path appeared a second young maiden, quite different from the first. She wore plain white garments and her eyes were grave, yet quiet, sweet and calm.

"My sister deceives you, Hercules," said she. "The pleasant things offered you down below are not worth the having. They are toys of which you will tire in a day and must be bought with a price of which you little dream. Do not descend thither, but climb the mountain path with me. You will find it rough and difficult, 'tis true. Yet, breasting its heights, you will there find real delights of which you can never tire. Moreover, if you have the courage to climb, this road will lead you to Mt. Olympus itself and there you shall live forever with the gods who cannot die."

And then in his dream Hercules turned his back on the gay and laughing maiden and took the mountain road. Thus did he choose the labors by means of which he turned his strength to good account for men.

Now Hercules had a cousin named Eu-rys'theus, King of My-ce'nae, who was a few days older than he. It had therefore been decreed that Hercules should be the slave of Eurystheus and in all things serve and obey him. Only on condition that he successfully performed twelve tasks that Eurystheus should set him, could he ever again be free. When Hercules presented himself at the court of King Eurystheus, he was already remarkable for his broad shoulders and the enormous muscles of his arms, while Eurystheus was miserably puny, timid, frail and weak. When Eurystheus for the first time beheld his powerful cousin, he was terrified at his strength, and he resolved to set him the hardest and most dangerous tasks that wit of man could possibly devise.

At this time in a beautiful grove that surrounded the temple of Ju'pi-ter in Ne-me'a, a fierce lion had its den. This lion was laying waste the whole countryside, so the people lived in constant terror of its ravages. The first task which Eurystheus set Hercules was to kill the Nemean lion. The young man set out with only his bow and arrows for weapons, but as he journeyed along, he found a sturdy olive tree by the roadside. With a single wrench, he pulled up the whole stout tree by its roots and made himself a club.

As he drew nearer the lion's haunts, nowhere did he meet with man, woman or child, for all had been so terrified, that they kept within doors, leaving their flocks to its mercy. At length Hercules came to the beautiful grove by the Temple of Jupiter and there he watched all day long. Towards night the lion came creeping home to its lair. It was a tremendous creature, fierce and terrible. Hercules twanged his bow and sent an arrow flying. The arrow struck the beast, but so tough was its hide that the sharp point glanced aside and fell harmless. The lion snarled, showed its fierce teeth, and looked about for its foe. A second arrow Hercules shot, but it glanced aside like the first. Ere he could shoot a third, the lion had espied him. It crouched and sprang straight at his throat. Hercules knocked it aside with a powerful blow from his club, then as it rose ramping and clawing the air, he seized its neck with both hands and hung on fast till he slew it.

His first task thus accomplished, Hercules went back to Eurystheus, wearing the skin of the lion over his shoulder while the head of the beast rested on his own like a kind of helmet. Henceforth Hercules was always to be distinguished by the lion's skin which he wore and the enormous club which he carried. When he came in such fashion into Eurystheus' presence, the coward was as frightened as though he had suddenly seen the Nemean lion itself before him. Yet when he was somewhat calmed he said:

"Hercules has slain the Nemean lion, 'tis true, still, the lion was but a beast after all. I will send him now to dispose of a hideous monster."

So he sent for Hercules and bade him kill the powerful Ler'ne-an hydra. This hydra was a tremendous serpent with nine heads, one of which was immortal and could not possibly be slain. It had its den near a fountain that supplied all the region about with water and it drove the unfortunate peasants away, so they had no means whatever whereby to slake their thirst.

Hercules took with him his young nephew I'o-laus, and off they started. In an oozy, evil-smelling marsh, they found the hydra, twisting its nine ugly heads in the air and breathing forth poison. Hercules made at it at once, but whenever he cut off a head, two grew in its place, so at every stroke it only became more formidable.

"Ho, Iolaus, set fire to yon grove of young trees," cried Hercules, "and keep me supplied with the burning brands."

Then he applied a brand to the neck wherever he cut off a head, and so prevented the new heads from growing. At length the immortal head alone was left. This Hercules had cleaved from the body, but it still spit its venomous poison as fiercely as before. So Hercules rolled a huge rock over it, and left it buried deep where it could never do further harm.

Now when Eurystheus found that his cousin had slain the hydra as well as the lion, he began to think there was no evil creature that Hercules could not kill.

"But," he mused, "his third task shall be harder still. After all it is no great task to kill. I shall bid him bring me *alive* the fierce Er-y-man'thi-an boar."

Accordingly he gave orders, and off went Hercules as before. Straight to Mt. Erymanthus he went and struggled long with the famous wild boar, but he caught him at length with his naked hands and brought him back on his shoulders. When King Eurystheus saw Hercules coming home with the boar alive on his shoulders, he was so badly frightened that he ran and jumped into a great bronze

pot in one corner of his palace, pulling down the cover in haste to keep himself well out of sight. He did not run so quickly however, but that Hercules caught just a glimpse of him as the cover went banging down.

"Ho, ho!" he cried out gravely, but with a twinkling eye, "this pot is just the place in which to keep a boar that is like to tear men to pieces." And he quickly lifted the lid and popped in the boar on top of the King. Loud was the outcry, you may be sure, till Hercules dragged out the two, the King in one hand, the boar in the other, both kicking, struggling, roaring!

"His strength seems equal to any deed," said Eurystheus to

himself, "yet will I get the best of him this time by setting a task that demands not strength, but fleetness of foot, and superhuman endurance." Then he summoned Hercules to him and bade him bring him alive the stag of Di-an'a. This stag had often befooled the hunters of that region. It was most marvelously fleet of foot and few had ever seen it. But report had said it had horns of gold, and hoofs of brass. It could make the most wonderful leaps and was never wearied, no matter how long the dogs might have chased it. It had been seen browsing oftener than else-where close to the steps of Diana's Temple, and many people be-lieved it was under the protection of that goddess.

So Hercules set out for the Temple of Diana, and watched and waited patiently. At last it appeared,—the golden antlered creature, a sight of wondrous beauty. Every muscle a-quiver it stood, cautious and alert, ready to dart away at the slightest whisper of danger.

Hercules sprang towards it at once. It gave a mighty leap and made off, swift as the flying wind. But Hercules made after it, hot on its heels. Over hill, over dale it flew, through forest and meadow, over shallow stream and broad deep river, on and on and on. A whole year long it ran, over nearly the whole of Europe, and a whole year long Hercules followed, till at last he wearied it out, and it fled back, exhausted and panting, to seek shelter in Diana's Temple. Even there Hercules would have seized it, but just then a flood of silver light shone gently round about, and there before him appeared a lovely lady in short white garments, with a bow and quiver at her back and a half moon on her crown. It was Diana herself, goddess of the moon and of the chase, and to her the stag ran trembling.

"You must not lay hands on this stag," she said. "It belongs to me. But return to King Eurystheus, and tell him how your endurance has wearied it out and how but for me you would have had it. I promise you he shall consider that your fourth labor is accomplished."

Now Eurystheus was almost at a loss how further to test such a Hercules, but he thought: "I have tried his strength, his endurance and agility. I will now try his wits, and send him on an adventure that only the devising of some skillful plan can ever accomplish."

In the valley of Stym-pha'lus there had come an enormous flock of strange birds that did great damage to crops and herds, and even carried off children. These birds had claws of iron, and feathers of metal, sharp at the end, which they had the power of throwing down on their enemies. No fleetness of foot, endurance, or bodily strength could dispose of such foes as these, that could not be prevented from darting up into the air out of reach. So Eurystheus bade Hercules save the valley of Stymphalus from these ugly birds. Hercules wisely decided at once not to fight with such creatures. Instead, he went quietly into the deep dark wood where they had their nests by the side of a noisome pool. Holding his bronze shield above his head to protect himself from their feathers, he rang a great bell and at the same time beat on his shield with his lance. Frightened at this hideous noise the birds flew up in such numbers that they darkened all the sky. As they flew over Hercules' head, their feathers fell fast like hail on his shield, but he continued to ring the bell and beat the shield till every one of the birds had disappeared from the place, so frightened by the noise that none ever dared return.

Thereafter, Eurystheus set Hercules five well-nigh impossible labors more. First, he must clean out in one day the filthy stables of King Au-ge'as wherein the King had kept three thousand oxen for thirty years without ever cleansing their stalls. The refuse was piled mountain high, but Hercules dug a trench, turned the waters of two great rivers through the stables and cleaned them

thoroughly in one day. Then he must fetch to Mycenae alive the raging white bull of Crete, but he seized it by its horns and held it so firmly in spite of its terrible struggles that the bull saw it had met its master and followed him like a lamb. For his eighth labor he captured the savage man-eating horses of King Di-o-me'des; for the ninth he brought back the girdle of Hip-pol'y-ta, Queen of the Am'a-zons, a fierce tribe of war-like women who were never defeated in battle; for the tenth he overcame the giant Ger'y-on with his three great bodies, his three great heads, and six arms that waved like a windmill.

When Hercules always succeeded, his cousin was in despair. For his eleventh labor, Eurystheus set him what he deemed the most impossible task of all. He bade him never again show his face in Mycenae unless he brought back three golden apples from the Garden of the Hes-per'i-des, for he knew full well that no man on earth knew where to find that garden. But Hercules would not be daunted. He set out to westward where the sky glows golden at sunset. There, thought he, behind that golden gate should lie such a garden of golden fruit. He journeyed long and he journeyed far, but at last he came to a beautiful spot on the banks of a river, where a band of graceful river nymphs played hide and seek mid the rocks. As soon as they perceived the hero, they ran laughing, with ropes of flowers, to seize him and make him their prisoner. Then they led him into a shady beech grove, where they bade him sit on a grassy knoll and offered him refreshment of luscious purple grapes. But Hercules would not linger.

# THE TREASURE CHEST

He begged the nymphs to tell him where lay the Garden of the Hesperides of which he was in search.

"You must seek out Pro'te-us, the Old Man of the Sea," they told him. "He knows every land whereon the ocean laps, but he will never tell you this secret unless you compel him. You must catch him and hold him fast no matter what may happen until he tells you the truth."

Thanking the nymphs for their kindness, Hercules again set out. He followed the river on and on till he heard the mighty boom of the sea. Then he advanced cautiously to the shore and there he saw fast asleep, lulled by the roar of the waters, a little old man whose hair and beard flowed down like a tangle of sea-weed. Here, for certain, was the Old Man of the Sea himself and no doubt at all about it. So Hercules stepped forward, quickly

seized him by an arm and a leg, and held him fast.

"Tell me," he cried, "where lies the Garden of the Hesperides."

Proteus awoke in a fright, and the next instant Hercules found he was holding in his hands no little old man, but a struggling stag. The change was astounding enough but still Hercules held on tight. Then the stag became a sea bird screaming to be free, the sea bird changed to a fierce three-headed dog, the three-headed dog to a savage giant, the giant to a monstrous snake. But the more terrifying were the forms which the old man assumed, the tighter Hercules held him. At last perceiving that Hercules could not be frightened into letting him go, Proteus appeared in his own rightful form once more and told him the truth.

"Go down into Africa," he said, "where the giant At'las holds up the sky and Atlas will get the apples for you."

So Hercules set out for Africa, but he had scarcely touched the African shore, when he was attacked by the terrible giant, An-tae'us who let no man pass him alive. This giant was son of the earth, and the most difficult of all giants to conquer, for whenever he was knocked down, he gained fresh strength from the dust and sprang up stronger than ever. But Hercules, knowing it was from the earth his strength had come, lifted him high above his head and held him there, struggling and kicking, separated from the source of his power, till the life was crushed out of him. Then he went again on his way.

Being wearied somewhat by the struggle, he soon lay down for a little rest and fell asleep. Suddenly he awoke, feeling as if he had been stung by a thousand insects. As he sat up and rubbed his eyes, what should he see about but a multitude of Pygmies,—

tiny people, no larger than bumble bees, who had climbed up over his body and attacked him with their tiny bows and arrows. Another man might have been angered by their little teasing stings, but Hercules only laughed with a loud resounding guffaw, whereat the Pygmies all ran away, save a very few that Hercules caught in his hand, and tied up in a corner of his lion's skin to take back home to Eurystheus.

After this Hercules wandered on and on till he saw looming up before him,—a mountain it looked to be, yet it was only a giant so tall that the clouds hung about his face like a beard and drifted around his shoulders. He was holding up his hands and on these and his head he bore the blue dome of the sky. At last, here was Atlas, and Hercules, nothing daunted by the fearful weight of the heavens under which even Atlas groaned, offered to relieve the giant by bearing the burden himself, if Atlas would get for him three golden apples from the Garden of the Hesperides. Atlas was more than willing, for the nymphs who guarded the apples were his nieces and to him the adventure was nothing more than a holiday. So Hercules climbed a mountain nearby to be of the giant's height, took the sky on his shoulders, and bore its tremendous weight while Atlas went off for the apples.

In due time back came the giant, but so much had he enjoyed his holiday, that he sought by a trick to give Hercules the slip and leave him forever with the sky on his shoulders. Hercules saw through the trick, however, outwitted the clumsy fellow, and made safely off with the apples.

Now that Hercules had accomplished eleven of the twelve labors, Eurystheus was beside himself. He could think of only

one task more that it seemed no man could ever achieve. He would send Hercules down into the under-world, the dark and gloomy abode of Plu'to, to bring thence the hideous three-headed watch-dog Cer'ber-us. Who that had entered those gloomy gates had ever been known to return? This would of a certain be the end of Hercules, for here, men said, was the abode of death.

Hercules journeyed away till he came to a deep chasm between two black and frowning rocks. Far, far below gleamed waters black as ink and now and again strange rumblings as of thunder shook the earth. Here was the only entrance to the under-world. Still Hercules knew no fear. Down into the deep black hole he climbed. There before him guarding the way, he saw Cerberus with his three savage heads and his tail like a snake. The dog let him enter readily. It would be when he sought again to go out that the creature would make at him.

Straight to Pluto's throne through the dark and dreary shadows went Hercules without once turning aside. Of Pluto himself he demanded permission to carry his watch-dog back to Mycenae. Pluto was struck with his daring.

"Hercules," said he, "you have done and suffered much, and proved yourself a true hero. Go, therefore. You shall take my watch-dog back if you can conquer him barehanded."

So Hercules returned once more to the gate. There stood Cerberus, no more quiet, but bristling with rage, showing his savage teeth, and crouching ready to spring. Hercules lost no time. He seized the dog on the spot with his vice-like grip, and dragged him straight off to Eurystheus.

When Eurystheus saw this remarkable sight, when he saw that Hercules had conquered even death and come back from that under-world whence men said none could ever return, he at once set his cousin free. At length the terms of his bondage had all been fulfilled. Nevertheless, Eurystheus strictly forbade Hercules ever again to enter the gates of Mycenae.

Thereafter, Hercules, now at last his own master, wandered over the earth ridding the world of many a monstrous evil and doing mighty deeds for the good of all mankind. When the end of his earth journey came, he laid himself down on a funeral pyre and bade men set it aflame. Bright purifying flames sprang leaping up about him. All that could ever die they burned away. Then the real Hercules, the immortal Hercules came out from the fire all shining and glorious. A rainbow appeared in the sky. Lo! it was Iris' bridge that led from earth to heaven. A moment after the clouds broke away; Iris in all her shimmering colors appeared and Mercury with his winged shoes. Over the rainbow bridge they led the immortal Hercules, as the maid of his dream had promised, to Mt. Olympus itself, there to live forever among the gods with all who are truly heroes.

## Thor's Journey to Jo'tun-heim
### A Norse Myth

WHEN the lightning leaps from cliff to cliff across the sky, and the thunder roars and rumbles, reverberating, rolling, crashing, then is the brazen chariot of Thor, the Thunderer, rolling and rattling over the heavens;—thus said the Norsemen, sons of the Northland. From the hoofs of the goats that draw his chariot fly blazing sparks, about his head gleams a crown of burning flame. In his strong right hand he grips his red hot hammer, Mjol'ner, from whence spring thunderbolts. It is against the great frost giants who dwell in Jo'tun-heim that Thor makes war—the giants who send forth ice and snow and bitter winds to nip the tender buds and kill the flowers; who wrap the earth in wintry mists and ruin harvests by their tempests.

It happened once that the storm giants held the earth too long in bondage. Frozen lay the rivers, and frozen the earth till long past the time for the coming of swallows, and no man could till the ground or plant the tender seed. Then from far off Asgard where dwell the gods, came Thor, Thor, the friend of farmers, Thor, the Deliverer, to do battle with the giants.

At the close of day Thor and Lo'ki, his companion, came to a cottage on the edge of a wood. Then rapped Thor on the door with his iron gauntlet, and called those within to give them food and shelter. Shelter the poor people gladly gave but food they had not to offer. So Thor raised his hammer and slew his own goats to serve for their supper. Amazed stood the poor peasants before him, but thus spake Thor:

"Eat, eat what ye will! Only heed this command,—break no single one of the bones, but cast them all when ye have finished into the skins on the floor."

Then Thor ate his fill, and Loki likewise, and the peasant, and his wife, and Thi-al'fi, their son, and Rosk'va, their daughter. But Thi-al'fi, the greedy one, secretly broke a bone, to come at the sweet, juicy marrow; then he cast the pieces onto the skin with the rest of the bones. Early on the morrow up rose Thor from his couch and over the goats' skins and bones flourished good Mjol'ner, his hammer. Lithe and light, lively and brisk, up sprang the goats, handsome and whole as before. Only one, alas! limped as he ran. Then Thor knew that some one had disobeyed him. Dark grew his brow as the storm cloud; he raised his powerful hammer and all stood about in terror.

"Some one has disobeyed me!"

On his knees fell Thi-al'fi before him confessing his fault, and such was his sorrow and terror that Thor relented and let his hammer fall harmless.

"Rise," he said, "but for thy fault thou and thy sister Rosk'va shall follow me henceforth and be my servants forever."

Then did Thor leave his chariot and his goats in the charge of the peasant, bidding him give them good care against his return, and he set off once more with Lo'ki, Thi-al'fi and Rosk'va on foot for the realm of the giants. All day through a bleak and desolate land they journeyed into a land of mist and fog and gloom. At nightfall they sought for a shelter. Before them out of the mist loomed dim outlines of a house. They entered a spacious doorway, broad and high. Within was no one, neither fire, nor light, nor food. Flinging themselves wearily on the floor, Thor and his companions fell asleep.

Not long had they slept when a strange trembling shook the earth and awoke them,—a roar and long drawn rumbling.

"It is an earthquake!" cried Thi-al'fi. Thereat Thor sent Loki and the others for safety into an inner room that seemed to be one of five branching off from the outer hall, while he himself stood guard at the door. When day began to dawn, lo! he saw through the mist a tremendous giant lying near and he perceived that the

upheaval which they had thought an earthquake the night before was but the noise of his snoring! Boldly he approached the giant.

"Awake!" he cried, "and tell me who thou art."

"Who be I?" cried the giant, stretching and looking about. "Skry'mir, my little fellow,—Skry'mir, the giant,—that's who I be. But where hast thou taken my mitten?"

At that Thor perceived that the house wherein they had slept was naught but the giant's glove! He called his comrades to come forth and out they stepped from the thumb! Loudly guffawed the giant.

"Ho, ho! little ones!" laughed he. "Where do ye journey? Whither away so bold?"

When he heard they were traveling to Jo'tun-heim he offered to be their guide. All day long they journeyed and all day long did Skry'mir belittle them and make them believe themselves good-for-naught. At nightfall, ere he dropped off to sleep, he offered them whatever food they might wish to take from the great pro-vision bag that hung on his shoulder. But when they tried to open the bag, not all four together, as Skry'mir had known full well, could unfasten the knots by which the giant had tied it. Then was Thor sorely wroth that Skry'mir should make them appear such weaklings, and he raised his hammer and dealt him a fearful blow on the forehead. The giant opened one sleepy eye.

"Was that a leaf fell on me?" said he.

A second time Thor lifted his hammer and hurled it with all his force at the head of the giant. But Skry'mir only murmured: "Methought an acorn dropped on my head."

Now Thor put forth such strength as never he knew he had, and smote the giant on the temple. "There must be birds over-head," said Skry'mir. "A feather just now tickled me."

Then did Thor go back to his comrades. Early on the morrow, Skry'mir pointed out the shortest road to Jo'tun-heim, and then took leave of his fellows. But first he said: "O Thor, I would give thee advice. Think not to stand up against the mighty ones

whom thou wilt find in Jo'tun-heim. Prepare to bow thyself rather before them, for I be the smallest among them!"

In spite of his words, on went Thor, and soon there before him and his comrades loomed up a glittering city of ice, with spires and pinnacles of icicles. So high it was that they had to bend back their heads to see its top. Slipping between the enormous bars of the gate, the travellers presented themselves in the great hall before Ut'gard-lo'ki, the King of the Giants about whom, on benches, sat his tremendous followers.

"Oho!" cried the King of the Giants, squinting contemptuously down as if at some little fly on the floor, which he could scarcely discover. "Whom have we here? Little Thor, as I live, out of Asgard. I have heard thou art small, but in truth I had never thought so small! 'Tis said thou hast strength, though, and can perform many great exploits! I scarce can believe it! Yet come, let us see what thou and thy comrades can do against my giants. Choose your own feat. At what will ye first contend?"

Then cried Lo'ki who had fasted long enough to feel great hunger: "In eating will I contend with any man among ye."

A great platter of meat the King ordered into the hall, and summoned his servant, Lo'gi, to contend with Lo'ki. Lo'ki sat himself at one end of the platter and Lo'gi at the other and both began to eat. Like an honest man an-hungered, ate Lo'ki, but when he was come to the center of the platter, there he met Lo'gi, and while Lo'ki had eaten but the meat, the giant had devoured meat and bones and platter as well!

"Not much can ye do at eating!" scornful, cried Ut'gard-lo'ki.

Then did Thor, nettled and keenly athirst, offer to outdo anyone at drinking. Immediately was brought a horn which the King declared strong men emptied at one draught, weaker men at two and the veriest weaklings at three. Eagerly Thor applied his lips to the rim. But though he drank long and deep,

440

the water seemed not to grow less by so much as a hair's breadth. Again he tried and again. The horn remained ever full.

"Not much can ye do at drinking," scornful, cried Ut'gard-lo'ki.

Then cried Thi-al'fi that he would run a race with any among the giants. Came one named Hu'gi, and, though Thi-al'fi kept hot on his heels in three different races, Hu'gi ever outstripped him.

"Not much can ye do at running," scornful, cried Ut'gard-lo'ki.

Next shouted Thor that he would contend in lifting.

"Lift me then my house cat," cried the King. " 'Tis a trifling game at which we only exercise children. I should never propose it to Thor save that I have found him so puny a little stripling."

Angrily, Thor seized the cat. At first he could not budge her. Then he arched her back from the ground, then he lifted one mighty paw. The faces of the giants turned pale, still Ut'gard-lo'ki called, "Not much can ye do at lifting!"

Last of all, cried Thor in a fury: "Let me contend at wrestling."

"My poor old nurse, El'li, belike is a fit match for thee," jibed the King and into the hall came a feeble old hag, weak-seeming and bent nearly double. Yet she seized Thor in a grip like a vise. Valiantly he struggled, but the more he tightened his hold, the firmer stood El'li, till at last she had him on his knees. Then cried Ut'gard-lo'ki: "No more will we contend. In truth ye are good for naught!"

On the morrow at daybreak, Thor and his comrades, sad and heavy hearted, set out once more for home. Ut'gard-lo'ki accompanied them outside the gates of the city. Once there, he cried: "How now, Thor, hast thou met mightier men than thou? Is it so easy as thou didst think to conquer the giants?"

"Nay," Thor made honest answer, "I have come off badly. My heart sinks with shame that I have proved such a weakling!"

Then was the King struck with the blunt and open truth of him who never yet uttered untruth, and he cried:

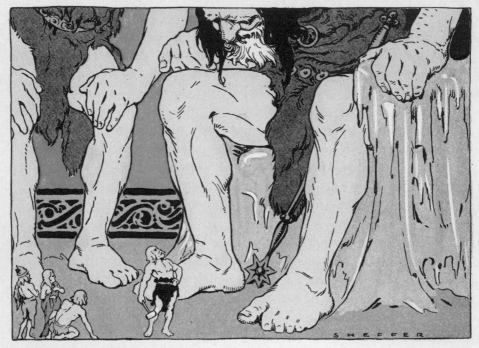

"O Thor, of Asgard, thou goest hence from my kingdom,—
forever and aye I trust, and now will I too speak the truth. Not
by superior force, as ye think have ye been defeated. It has all
been done by magic. All things have been made to seem to you
other than they were. Even have we made you think yourselves
weak and puny, when our very bones rattled for trembling and
fear of your strength. I myself am Skry'mir and any one of thy
mighty blows would have done for me, had I not in the mist,
which distorts all things out of their natural shape, made thee
believe a mountain my head. Not me didst thou strike but the
mountain. Lo'gi, against whom Lo'ki contended in eating, is wild-
fire, the devourer; Hu'gi, against whom Thi-al'fi ran, is thought,
and who can run faster than thought? The horn from which
thou, Thor, didst drink is connected with the ocean so thou

442

couldst never have drained it unless thou couldst drink dry the ocean. El'li, the wrestler, is old age, who throws so many strong men, and the cat thou couldst not lift is the Mid'gard serpent that encirles the world. Yet didst thou nearly outdo Lo'gi, Hu'gi and El'li and lift the Mid'gard serpent, and thou didst drink so much of the sea that on earth men thought the tide had gone out. By trickery only have we kept you from your triumph, but in trickery are we clever. If ye be wise come no more against us. With deception and illusion will we meet you always."

Then in his righteous wrath Thor lifted up his hammer. The might that was his, the power that was his, once more he knew. But as he swung good Mjol'ner, the giant vanished—vanished, too, the whole city of freezing ice and snow. Retreated had the giants before the power of Thor, perceived by them when to Thor himself his prowess had seemed so little. Fled had the giants before him. Then once more smiled the earth, free from the fetters of frost, ready for seed and bloom, and back to Asgard went Thor with Lo'ki, Thi-al'fi and Rosk'va.

## THOR

HENRY WADSWORTH LONGFELLOW

I am the God Thor,
I am the War God,
I am the Thunderer!
Here in my Northland,
My fastness and fortress,
Reign I forever!

Here amid icebergs,
Rule I the nations;
This is my hammer,
Mjolner, the mighty;
Giants and sorcerers
Cannot withstand it!

*—from The Saga of King Olaf.*

# The Stealing of I-du'na

### A Norse Myth

IT happened once that O'din, the All-father, King of the gods, with Hoe'nir, his brother, and Lo'ki, the mischief-maker, started out of As'gard, the home of the gods, down across the Bridge of the Rainbow, to journey around the world. At eventide they came to a densely wooded mountain, and being anhungered, yet finding no dwelling in sight, they caught an ox from a herd that stood grazing near and dressed the meat for their supper. Then did Lo'ki, god of fire, kindle a flame to cook the food, but the time being come for the meat to be done, lo! it was raw as in the beginning. Another fire made Lo'ki, but all in vain. As raw was the meat as before. Then Lo'ki, O'din and Hoe'nir heard a noise in the branches above them. Looking up they perceived an eagle fanning the meat with his wings and sending a cold wind upon it that prevented it from roasting.

"Done to a turn will your meat be," croaked the eagle, "if you will promise me as much as I can eat."

"Nay, then!" cried the three out of Asgard. "Join us and eat what thou wilt."

So the eagle left off fanning the meat; it was soon cooked and they all went to help themselves. But the eagle, first of all, seized three-quarters of the whole ox. Then was Lo'ki angered. Seizing a stick lying near, he began to belabor the greedy bird. No sooner had he done so, than one end of the pole stuck fast in the eagle's feathers, and the other stuck fast to Loki's hands. Up flew the bird and off trailed Loki after him. Scraped through briery thickets and straggling branches of trees, jammed against rocks and stones, his arms nearly torn from their sockets, so was Loki dragged. Then he knew that the eagle was in truth no eagle, but Thi-as'si, the fierce frost giant. In vain he begged for mercy. The bird flew on the faster. Again and again he begged.

"On one condition only will I let thee go," croaked Thi-as'si, "that thou lure out of Asgard the lovely I-du'na, and give her into my power with a dish of her magic apples, partaking of which keeps the dwellers in Asgard forever young."

At length Thi-as'si wrung from Loki the sorry promise to do as he bade him, and Loki was set free. Bedraggled and torn, back went Loki to Asgard.

Now I-du'na, Spirit of the Spring and of immortal youth, was loveliest of all the goddesses in Asgard. Tender green were her garments, on her head a wreath of flowers. Lightly she glided over the earth. At her approach the trees burst into bloom; myriads of flowers sprang up; tinkling brooks awoke and laughed and leapt for joy. Everywhere was stir, activity and life. Never was age where Iduna was, but always youth— eternal youth. And Iduna kept carefully guarded in her charge a tree that bore wonderful apples, which made him who ate them forever young. It was to partake of that eternal youth that the cruel frost giant wished to get possession of Iduna and her apples.

The husband of Iduna was Bra'gi, the god of poesy, who sings the wondrous song of life that scales the highest heavens and searches the depths of hell. Whenever he sings and plays on his golden harp, the flowers that spring up at Iduna's approach reveal their inmost charm and grace, the blending colors of earth and sky reveal their inmost harmony, the laughter of brooks, the songs of birds reveal their inmost joy; all nature finds a tongue and speaks and yields up the very secret of her being. To separate Iduna from Bragi was no easy task, but Loki waited until he saw the minstrel go forth on a journey from Asgard to earth, leaving Iduna unguarded. Then the mischief-maker went whither Iduna wandered alone in the midst of her flowery gardens.

"Iduna," said he, "just without the gates of Asgard I have found a tree that bears finer apples than thine. Sweeter to the taste are they and lovelier, and indeed I doubt not they restore youth and strength as well as thine."

"Nay, now," cried Iduna, "in all the world are none such apples as mine."

"Come then with me and see," said Loki. "And bring with thee a dish of thine own apples that we may compare the two."

Into a crystal dish did Iduna then put her precious apples and off with the wily Loki went she. Scarcely were the two without the safe protected gates of Asgard than Thiassi in his eagle plumage swooped down upon Iduna. As the storm swoops, as the storm rushes, when down from the mountain tops the wild north wind comes roaring, so came Thiassi. From his frosty wings fell snow, from his breath exhaled the cold that blasted all about. In his talons seized he Iduna and bore her off to his wintry home in the storm-bound land of Thrym'heim. There he shut her up in a chamber in the rocks, against which all day long resounded the boom and crash of the sea.

Each day he came and asked her to give him a bite of her apples, for not unless Iduna herself gave out the precious fruit would he who partook thereof find his youth and strength renewed. And every day Iduna stoutly refused. He whined and begged and threatened—in vain! For no such creature of evil was the gift of eternal youth. And when Thiassi himself thrust his great fist in the dish to seize an apple, the fruit only dwindled and shrunk till it disappeared altogether.

# THE TREASURE CHEST

Long were the days, long were the months while Iduna stayed in Thrymheim. In Asgard, the heavens, and Midgard, the earth, spring and summer were gone. Cold winter held sway; leaves turned brown and fell; bird songs were hushed; flowers withered and drooped on their stalks; brooklets froze up into motionless silence, and all things seemed old and dying. In Asgard old age came stealing even upon the gods. Where, O, where was Iduna? Bragi mourned for her, Odin mourned for her, mourned all the dwellers in Asgard, mourned all the people of earth.

Then did Odin, the All-father, summon a council to consider what should be done. Thither all Asgard gathered—save Loki. Loki dared not appear. When Odin perceived that Loki alone was absent, he ordered Bragi to fetch him the maker-of-mischief. In the presence of Odin, before the might of his majesty, Loki was forced to pour out the tale of what he had done. Sternly Odin bade him go and bring back Iduna or never more dare show his face in Asgard.

So Loki borrowed of the goddess Frey'a her cloak of falcon feathers, and with this he was able to fly over land and sea to the rockbound coast of Thrymheim. Here in her gloomy cell he found the lovely Iduna. Thiassi, it chanced, was from home, so Loki forced his way through a narrow opening into her prison. Much she rejoiced to see him. He turned her at once into a swallow and flew off with her in his talons.

447

Not far had he gone, when he heard a rushing behind him. There in rapid pursuit was Thiassi. On and on flew Loki! On and on flew Thiassi, gaining little by little. On the walls of Asgard stood the gods wrinkled, and bent, and gray, watching far to southward over the sea, watching, longing for the coming of Iduna. At length they made out the falcon, Loki, and Thiassi hot on his heels. Long and anxiously watched they. Now Thiassi seemed pouncing on Loki's back, but always Loki escaped and flew with his precious burden on and on and on.

As he neared the city of refuge Loki's strength seemed almost failing. Then up rose the dwellers in Asgard and lit great fires on the walls that leapt and flamed to the heavens. Safe through the blaze and smoke dashed Loki,—Loki the god of fire, but when Thiassi, creature of cold and storm, plunged blundering through, down he fell, suffocating, to his end beneath the mighty hammer of Thor. Then Loki let loose the swallow and up sprang the lovely Iduna herself, to be tenderly welcomed by Bragi, Odin and all the rest. And with Iduna and her apples, back to Asgard came youth and the joyous life of the Spring.

## HOW THE GODDESS OF SPRING CAME TO SCORING

CHARLES KINGSLEY

White were the moorlands,
And frozen before her;
Green were the moorlands,
And blooming behind her.
Out of her gold locks
Shaking the spring flowers,
Out of her garments
Shaking the south wind,
Around in the birches,
Awaking the throstles,
And making chaste housewives all,
Long for their heroes home;
Loving and love-giving,
Came she to Scoring.
—from The Longbeard's Saga.

448